Contents

EDITOR **CLAYTON HICKMAN**
DESIGNER **PERI GODBOLD**

FRONT COVER PAINTING BY **ALISTER PEARSON**
Dedicated to the memory of **Margaret Dedman**

FRONTISPIECE PENCILS BY **MIKE COLLINS**
INKS BY **DAVID A ROACH** COLOURS BY **JAMES OFFREDI**

CONTENTS PAGE ILLUSTRATION **BRIAN WILLIAMSON**

WITH THANKS TO **RUSSELL T DAVIES, DAVID TENNANT** & **BILLIE PIPER,
TOM SPILSBURY, SCOTT GRAY, IAN GRUTCHFIELD,
KATE BEHARRELL, RICHARD HOLLIS** & **HARRIET NEWBY-HILL**

A letter from the Doctor

Squirn City,
Squirn,
Galaxy 5,
Septadecimber 32-and-a-half.

Hello all!

Rose and I are on the planet Squirn right now. And we've got on the wrong side of the Squirns. Then again, what's the right side? The Squirns know but they're not letting on.

Just got time to dash off a quick note to anyone who's bought this book. If you're reading this in the shop, don't look now but that woman over there in the blue top, yes her, flicking through the angling magazines... Slitheen! And if you've stolen this book be careful. Pages 32 and 33 are alive, and very moral, so when you go to sleep they'll probably try to eat you. You have been warned.

I love story books. Particularly ones like this, with pictures of hideous, monstrous, withered creatures. And that's only the photos of the writers. Don't fancy yours much, dear reader.

But it's all in here. Adventures you'll never see on telly, but with all the scares and mystery, the happy and sad times that follow me and Rose round the universe. The first cat in hyperspace; the computer hiding a terrible secret; the diary of Jason, the ordinary boy who helped us save Earth from 'the wet puppy with no eyes'; even a bit of opera. This is how it all happened.

Right, gotta go. The Squirns have got Rose! I'm going to do something amazing to set her free, but you're just gonna have to imagine what it'll be...

Happy times and places,

The Doctor

Cuckoo-Spit

WRITTEN BY **MARK GATISS**   ILLUSTRATIONS BY **DARYL JOYCE**

June 18th 1975

I know you're meant to start diaries in January and that but I haven't got round to it so I'm starting now. Grandad got me this book for Christmas. It's not really a diary, just an old book with blank pages that are a funny colour like butter because they're so old. I kept it in my socks and pants drawer for ages cos it seemed too nice to write in. Then Dad said *Have you started that diary yet Jason?* and I said *no* and he said *Typical. It's like the Starship Enterprise again.* I

didn't know what Dad meant and then I remembered cos I used to have a model of the space ship off *Star Trek* that fired little yellow round things instead of phasers. It was brilliant and made of metal like a Dinky car. But I was scared I'd lose the little yellow plastic things if I fired them so I never did. Then I lost the bag of yellow things. So I suppose Dad meant you might as well use something or else what's the point?

Anyway, I've started because something STRANGE has happened. A boy at our school has disappeared. It's dead

weird and the police have been to school and everything. I don't know him well cos he's a year above me but his name is Chris Rutter.

It's very warm and it's PE tomorrow which makes me feel a bit fed up.

June 19th 1975

Dad says Mrs Thatcher will never be prime minister because people remember her as Thatcher Thatcher the milk snatcher but I'm not bothered about that because school milk is always warm and tastes sour anyway. I hope she doesn't because what would Mike Yarwood do then?

PE was horrible as usual. I wish we could just stay inside and read books but at least it's not cold. It was football but I just stayed near the edge of the field with Graham Cook talking about horror films. Mr Boyd kept shouting at us to get stuck in and then the ball hit me on the side of the face and it knacked and everyone laughed except Graham. Graham got my glasses out of the mud and wiped them on his shirt and I thought that was very kind. I really like Graham but <u>I AM NOT A PUFF OR ANYTHING.</u> We walked home and I had egg, beans and chips and Mum let me have it on my knee because *Superstars* was on.

After tea, Mr Greenacre from next door came round and said *Had we heard?* and Dad said *What?* and Mr Greenacre said *That Rutter kiddie's Mother's gone missing now.* Mum made a funny sound and said *It was awful* and then I went to bed.

June 26th 1975

I think the worst thing about PE is waiting for it. When I'm actually doing it it's not too bad and some things like running I'm quite good at but I hate the time before. I go all funny in my tummy and feel a bit sick. It's worst in History cos I can see out over the fields and know I'll have to go out there soon and I'd rather stay in with books on the Tudors and Stuarts. Sometimes I look out of the window and see people walking past the school gates very quickly and I think *They're grown up and don't have to go to school and I want to be them.* Except today someone wasn't racing past he was just standing there, looking in. Dad says you have to watch out for people who hang around outside schools cos they'll fiddle with you. I couldn't see the man's face properly but there was something wrong with it. It looked all mixed up. I think he was smiling but I couldn't tell and it was like there was a light coming out of his eyes. On Bonfire Night, Dad's friend George from work lit up a great big bit of stuff and I got him to write down what it was and it was called <u>magnesium ribbon</u> and it was bright like snow in the sunshine and we all had to look away cos it hurt to look at it. The light from the man's eyes was a bit like that.

When I looked down at a picture of King Charles getting his head cut off it went all blurry and there was a funny sound in my head like ringing. When I looked out of the window again the man was still there and there was someone with him. A boy I think. They were turning away from the school.

I walked home on my own cos Graham had Drama Club and it was Corned Beef Hash for tea

which I love. If you put HP Sauce in it, it stays in a big brown blob and floats about.

Dad said I could stay up later cos there was a good film on – *Where Eagles Dare* – but it had just started when the phone rang and it was Graham's Mum asking if he was round ours. Mum said *No* and then asked me if I'd seen him and I told her about Drama Club. When Mum came off the phone I said *What's up?* and she said Graham hadn't come home after school. Dad whistled in his teeth like he does and said *Expect that's another one.*

I went to bed feeling very worried about Graham. I fell asleep but I woke up thinking about the man outside the school gates with the funny face.

June 29th 1975
Graham is definitely missing. The police have been round and Graham's Mum and Dad have been crying their eyes out.

Usually on Saturdays me and Graham go down the Ramp where the lads with skateboards go but we're no good with skateboards so we go to the library and then sit in the long grass and make up stories. We found a big metal thing in the stream once that was off a tractor or something but we pretended it was a bit off a flying saucer and it was brilliant being all the soldiers and scientists who got killed by the monsters.

But Graham wasn't there today so I just went off on my own. It got hot and I felt a bit sticky so I took off my jumper and tied it round me. I went down the fields and there was cuckoo-spit on lots of the tall grass. If you don't know what it is, it looks like dribble and you find it on some kinds of grass. It looks yukky but Mr Caterson in Science told us what it really is and if you wipe away the spit stuff there's a little green insect inside that makes the frothy stuff to protect itself. I was going to have a look for the insect but then I heard a really really strange noise like an old car engine. It was coming from the field over the hedge so I went and had a look. That field used to have a bull in it and there's still a sign on the gate even though the bull's not there. There's a dead tree there as well all covered in ivy and I was dead shocked cos under the tree was a big blue thing like a hut with POLICE written on it at the top. The door to the shed was open and there was a man there looking at the ground. He was a thin man in a brown suit and the suit was all crumpled even though he had a tie on. He looked angry and said something about running out of time and then started rubbing some soil between his fingers. The soil was around a big hole in the ground and all the grass had gone. The soil was all black and hard like burnt Christmas cake.

Then there was a noise in the bushes and a girl came out. She was very pretty and had a big chest like that swimming teacher that came for just one term. She called the thin man "doctor" and said to come here. The man followed and so did I and then I saw something in the stream, just like that bit of tractor that me and Graham found but different. This was like a big ball, all metal and with burn marks on it like the bottom of Grandad's kettle. The ball was more like a pear drop shape than a ball and the pointy end was all cracked. I know what the man said next cos I listened very hard and remembered it and it was *The hull must have fractured on impact* and it sounded like something off the telly and I was excited. Then the girl said *Have we lost them?* And the doctor man said *No, they wouldn't get away from him* and then he took out a metal thing like a torch from his pocket and a blue light came out of it. It was

AMAZING. The blue light came out in a like a fan shape and the metal pear drop thing sort of sparkled. I think I made a noise cos the doctor man and the girl looked up so I ran home straight away cos I was frightened they had seen me.

When I got home Mum and Dad were really cross with me for going off on my own and Mum said *Do you want to end up like those other kids* and I asked if Graham had come home and she said *No*.

I wasn't hungry and I said I wanted to go to bed early and Dad said *He's sickening for something* but Mum kissed me and I went to bed. I wasn't tired though. I just wanted to think about the thin man and the girl and the pear drop thing and the blue light.

I looked up at the Spitfire that is hanging from a wire on the ceiling for a bit and then I heard a noise outside. It was getting dark but when I went to the window I could see that someone was standing on the other side of our garden fence. It was the man from outside school again and he was just in a jumper and trousers like anyone and

he was all orange from the street lamp but I couldn't
see his face properly and then he moved a bit and I
saw him properly and I stepped back from the window
and felt a bit sick. His face was like an ordinary
person's face but jumbled up cos his eyes and nose and
mouth didn't look like they belonged together, like in
that game Misfits. And then he moved back a bit and
someone else came out of the shadow and it was
Graham Cook.

I was going to shout for Mum and Dad but Graham
had that light coming from his eyes like the man had
before and it was even brighter. His face was all wrong
too and then there was that ringing sound again and I
felt funny.

But then a dog started barking and someone banged
a door not far off and Graham and the man went
away and I was glad. I shut the curtains and I put the
blanket over my head. I wanted to go to sleep but I
couldn't.

June 30th 1975

It was Sunday and nothing ever happens on Sunday –
except this one. Jimmy Savile was on the radio and the
kitchen was full of steam and the smell of cabbages
like it always is when Mum's cooking Sunday dinner. I
said I was going to play in the shed and Mum said that
was ok as long as I didn't wander off again. But as
soon as I was outside I did wander off again because I
wanted to find the thin man and the girl.

I ran down to the field where the bull used to be and
the blue shed was still there. I went right up to it this
time and put my hand on it. Even though it was made
of wood it felt really strange and it made a noise like
the bees in Mr Clary's garden up the road. The words
on it said it was a police box so that was all right and
I knew the man and the girl must be from the police
even though they didn't look like the ones on Z Cars.

I knew they wouldn't still be by the stream but I
went to check anyway and the pear drop thing wasn't
there any more. I didn't know what else to do so I sat
down in front of the blue shed and waited.

It was very warm and I think I must have fallen
asleep because suddenly the door of the shed opened
and I sort of fell back into it. The girl said Whoops
and caught me and then her and the thin man came
out of the shed and closed the door. The man looked
down at me and he was a bit scary even though he was
wearing sand shoes.

The girl said Hello and asked me what my name was
and I told her and then the man said Well Jason.
You'd better go home. It's not safe and the girl said
Too right.

I told them I needed to talk to the police because I
knew where Graham Cook was and the man said
Who? So I told them all about the people that have
gone missing and the man outside school with the light
coming out of his eyes and how Graham was with him
and it was all a bit scary. I DIDN'T CRY but the
pretty girl got down on the grass and gave me a cuddle
and that was nice because she smelled lovely.

And then the thin man put his hands in his pockets
and made a face like Mr Caterson in Science when he's
thinking very hard. He said They've moved fast and
the girl said Yes. I didn't know who they meant and I
was going to ask but then the girl said What're they
doing? And the man said Feeding.

And then the man crouched down and smiled at me and I felt a lot better and he said *I'm going to ask you to be very brave, Jason*. And I said I WAS brave and what did he want me to do? And then the girl said that her and the doctor (that was what he was, a doctor. A doctor and a policeman like Quincy) had been chasing a kind of animal. *A wild animal?* I asked her and she said *Yeah*. A dangerous animal that had got out of somewhere it should have stayed in and it would cause all sorts of trouble and try to eat people up. People like the man outside school and Graham Cook and me.

So I nodded and asked what did this have to do with being brave and the doctor policeman said *You're the bait, Jason.* And the girl Rose (she said her name just when I was going) she said I should get home for my lunch and that was funny cos only posh people say Lunch. But I got home and Mum didn't even know I hadn't been playing in the garden shed.

The doctor man and Rose had told me what to do and I told them where I lived so all I had to do was go to bed early. I put my head near the radiator and told Mum I felt poorly and she believed me when she felt my head and I went to bed dead early. But I didn't put my pyjamas on. I stayed in my going out clothes and sat on the bed for ages till it got really dark.

I could hear the telly downstairs all mumbly and then after *That's Life* finished Mum and Dad came to bed. I knew Mum

would look in on me so I got under the covers and pretended to be asleep.

When the clock said Twelve twenty one I heard that ringing sound again in my head and I got out of bed and went to the window.

I saw Graham straight away and even though his face was all scrunched up I didn't feel as frightened cos Rose and the doctor policeman were outside too. So I did what the doctor had asked me to do and went downstairs <u>very quietly</u> and went out through the back door.

It was quite warm but I put on my parka cos I didn't know where I might be going and I walked up the path to the gate. Graham was standing under the street light and the orange of it made him look all blotchy. I said *Hello Graham* but he didn't say anything. His skin was all soft looking like when an apple's gone bad. I looked about for the doctor and Rose but I couldn't see them and then the ringing in my ears got worse like when you're having gas at the dentist's. Then there was the light in Graham's eyes like the Magnesium ribbon and he held out his hand and I took it. It should have been warm but it was all cold and scratchy like wet sand and I felt a bit sick.

And then it really was like the dentist's cos everything was all dark around me and I felt like everything was falling on top of me. I thought *You mustn't go to sleep cos it's a wild animal that's got Graham and made him go funny and it'll get you too* but it was no good cos the ringing got worse and worse and then I couldn't see anything any more.

I knew I was in someone's house when I woke up but it looked really strange and it smelled bad. A bit like the mucky water at the bottom of the toothbrush mug in our bathroom. There were no lights on but the Magnesium light was coming from somewhere and that's how I could see. And there were loads of people all lying on the carpet. It was like a grown up film I once saw a bit of on BBC2 where everyone's got drunk at a party and they fall asleep on the floor. Or something.

There was a lady lying near me and she seemed to be asleep only her eyes were wide open and her face looked soft like Graham's did.

My mouth was all dry and I had a very bad headache but I thought I was ok. I got frightened suddenly though because the doctor man and Rose weren't there and I could see Graham moving about in the kitchen. I sat up and tried to move really really slowly across the carpet. I couldn't see what Graham was doing but I knew it wouldn't be very nice.

Then something went wrong cos I tried to stand up and I felt all funny like I'd been in the sun too long and I sort of

half fell over. I tried to stop myself and my hand touched the face of the lady on the floor and my hand went RIGHT THROUGH her and I could feel the wet carpet underneath with my fingers. Her face just sort of crumbled away and it was like bubbles or foam on the sea and then I saw that there was something inside the lady and all the foam and stuff had been hiding it. It was a little thing like a puppy. A sort of wet puppy with no eyes and no mouth. Just a sort of shape and it had lots of legs like a centipede and it was a sort of rusty colour like dried up blood and its legs were wriggly. And then I think I must have been a real nancy because I think I screamed.

Then Graham came through from the kitchen and he was sort of smiling but it was all wrong and now I knew he was made of soft stuff. I was really scared and I went backwards on my bum towards the sofa but Graham kept coming towards me and I saw what was in his hands and it was one of the puppy things. Then I felt cold all over because I knew Graham was going to let it get me.

I looked down at the one that was in what was left of the lady and I suddenly thought *It's cuckoo spit. That's it.* The people like Graham and the lady and the man at the school gates, they're not real anymore. They're just to protect the little thing that's got in them. The real ones have been eaten up. And then I wished I'd been able to tell the doctor man and the nice girl because they'd know how clever I'd been but now it was too late and the wet thing with no eyes was going to get me and I was going to Heaven.

And then the white light in Graham's eyes went out all of a sudden because another light came on and it was from the end of the doctor man's torch. It covered the whole floor like a blanket and I had to close my eyes. And when I opened them again there was fire all over the place. Then Rose came running across the carpet and she lifted me up and she said *It's alright sweetheart* and *Thank God you're alright.* And I said I was alright but there were these things on the floor and they were horrible.

I looked down and saw that the fire was burning the puppy things and even though they didn't have any mouths they were sort of screaming cos I could hear it my head and it was awful. Then the doctor pointed

his torch at Graham Cook and Graham just sort of fell to bits like a snowman and the thing in his hands hit the floor and the puppy thing inside Graham fell out as well and the fire got them both.

I said *It's like Cuckoo spit* and Rose smiled then the doctor man got us out of the house and it turned out to be the farmhouse near the field where the bull used to be. We watched for a bit and the house burned down.

Then they took me back home and I was ok by now and it was <u>really</u> late but Mum and Dad were still asleep and we got back inside without them knowing.

Rose put me into bed and stroked my face and that was lovely. The doctor was standing by the window and I said that Rose had said the things in the house were wild animals and he said *Yes*.

But not like from Africa or anything? Noooo he said and he dragged out the word like that. They were from much farther away.

Then I was very sleepy and Rose told me to shut my eyes and not think about it anymore but I asked her about Graham and she said it was terrible but Graham had gone and all those other people in the house too but it was best not to talk about it. I said I wouldn't and then I told the doctor man about the Cuckoo spit and he said *Yes!* And that I was very clever and then I went to sleep.

July 1st 1975

The next day was meant to be school but I must have looked really poorly cos Mum let me have the day off and Grandad came to look after me. In the afternoon I had Oxtail soup and Grandad fell asleep when *Crown Court* was on so I got dressed and went out to the field. The blue shed wasn't there any more but there was a square where it had been and the grass was all white and flat like combed hair.

Later on, Mr Greenacre from next door came round and said *Have you heard?* and Dad said *What?* and he said they'd found the farmhouse all burned and there were some bits of bodies in there but not much and they were all changed and no one could explain it.

I could. But I'll never tell cos Rose and the doctor policeman asked me not to and I really liked them so I never will.

THE END

The Cat Came Back

WRITTEN BY **GARETH ROBERTS**   ILLUSTRATIONS BY **MARTIN GERAGHTY**

MITZI WAS GETTING HUNGRY.

She was in a tiny dark space, standing upright, and there was something across her body that held her still no matter how hard she struggled. Thin strands of cold wire were attached to her head, her stomach and her paws. She cried out for attention but nobody came.

She remembered being taken from the humans that fed her and then given a sharp pain in her side. When she woke, she was inside this dark metal box, and soon afterwards there'd been a tremendous, terrible noise and a lurching sensation that made her dizzy. Unnatural lights and strange colours that were not part of the world she knew – even the cold, electric human world – dazzled her.

But even that was better than this darkness. The hunger was getting sharper. She struggled harder. She had to escape, get food, or she would…

A strange new thought entered her head. Food stopped hunger, she knew that, it was obvious. But the new thought said that if you didn't stop hunger, you would die. *Dying?* Mitzi had always known about pain and trying to stop it, but dying – that was new. It meant you were going to stop living. But what was living?

As these new ideas whirled round her head, Mitzi suddenly realised something else. The thing holding her down was a strap, pulled tight across her stomach. All she had to do was unstrap it and she would be free. So she strained her front paws until they reached the catch, extended her claws and opened it. Then she

sprang up out of her dark confinement, the wires snapping free. Irritated, she gave herself a good lick and then looked around for something to eat.

The first thing she noticed was a window set higher up on one side of the box. She hurried over and sprang up on to the sill. The view was not what you'd expect from a window. There were no trees or birds. It was like the night sky out there. She'd never paid much attention to the night sky before, but she knew the stars were not normally as bright or as close as this.

More thoughts came tumbling into her mind. It was exhilarating. Every second she realised and understood new things. How could she have been so stupid before?

She was in space. The humans had trapped her and sent her up into space in this stupid box, to test their scientific equipment on her before they risked it on themselves. Then they'd abandoned her, without food, air or toilet facilities. A wave of anger rippled through her and she arched her back, her fur bristling, and spat.

'How dare they?!' she said.

Saying things. That was new too.

🌐   🌐   🌐

THE DOCTOR PRESSED 'ENTER' ON THE KEYBOARD built into the TARDIS console, and a new image flashed on to the monitor screen above. 'There they are,' he told Rose. 'The Great

Hyperspace Pioneers.'

The screen showed a slowly revolving black metal sphere covered in glowing pinpoints of light. It hovered over a huge green planet like an extra moon. 'There are people inside that?' asked Rose.

'Heroes inside that,' said the Doctor. 'The first humans to travel through hyperspace, they're out further than any human's been before. Apart from you, obviously. That's the planet Phostris, in the galaxy RE 461. They volunteered, risked their lives, to get here. Brave people. Spreading humanity's innovations through the universe.'

'One more question,' asked Rose. 'Hyperspace...?'

'Space is a B road, hyperspace is a motorway,' the Doctor replied, moving round the console to adjust various levers and switches. 'Gets you where you want to go very, very fast. But you have to punch a hole in space to get on it, and punch another one to get off it, that's tricky when you're just starting out like they are.' He nodded to the screen, his hand on a big lever. 'Shall we go and say well done?'

☺ ☻ ☺

ROSE TOOK A DEEP BREATH AND stepped through the police box doors on to deep sea-green carpet. Moulded foam couches were placed around a coffee table strewn with magazines, and a big window down one side looked down on to the planet. Framed pictures of Earth landscapes – desert, rolling French countryside, Indian mountains – were dotted along the curved walls. There was nothing cramped or makeshift about the place.

'What's this, Club Class?' she asked the Doctor.

'Crew room,' he replied, picking up and leafing through one of the magazines. 'Done it out nice, haven't they?'

Rose smiled. 'Dunno what's brave about staying here.' She pointed to a sun bed in a corner. 'Are these pioneers like, "ooh, shall I risk a tan today?"'

The room juddered.

The Doctor dropped the magazine. 'Sounds like a stabilizer misfiring.' He hurried from the room through a sliding door and Rose followed into a curved metal corridor. 'And where is everyone? There was a crew of twenty on all these early missions, and the sphere's not that big –'

Another door slid open automatically and the Doctor crashed to a halt. Over his shoulder, Rose saw a young man with close-cropped hair wearing a crumpled blue uniform with a name badge reading JONAH. He was sat cross-legged, head bowed as if in meditation. Then he looked up, and there was fear in his eyes.

'Don't worry, we're friends,' Rose said automatically.

The young man swallowed convulsively. 'What are you doing here?' he asked in a dry, croaking voice.

'Er, we're diplomats, official observers, come to say congrats,' said the Doctor, reaching in his pocket for his psychic paper.

But it didn't look as if he was going to need it. The young man licked his cracked lips and said urgently, 'Get back. Go home, if you still can. She might not know you're here yet. Go!' He gestured back down the corridor. 'And warn Earth!'

'We're not the going home type,' said the Doctor.

Rose leant down. 'Where are the others?'

Jonah shook his head. 'She got them.'

'Who's "she"? The cat's mother?' asked the Doctor.

Jonah stood up and backed away. 'Don't say that word, don't say that word!'

Rose followed him. 'Which word? "The?" "Mother?" "Cat?"'

'Don't say it!'

The sphere juddered again, this time knocking the Doctor, Rose and Jonah off their feet. The Doctor grabbed Rose's hand as the vibrations lessened and they pulled themselves upright.

'That's not a technical fault,' said the Doctor, suddenly serious. 'Something knocked us. Something's playing with us.'

Rose looked towards Jonah. He'd pressed himself against the wall, shaking his head and sobbing. She was about to reach out and comfort him when his entire body became suffused with a throbbing blue light. 'He's teleporting!' She thought again as the light formed a cone and disappeared taking Jonah with it as the ship shook once more. 'No. He's been teleported.'

'Right, come on, take us too!' the Doctor shouted into the air.

Rose couldn't resist joining in. 'Yeah, we're not frightened!'

The Doctor raised an eyebrow. 'We're not?'

'Well, I'm not if you're not.'

'And I'm not if you're not,' said the Doctor. 'I think that makes sense.' He shouted up again. 'Come on. Cat!'

A second later and Rose felt a strange tugging sensation in the pit of her stomach, blue light dazzled her, and then she was falling…

🌐 🌐 🌐

THE NEXT THING ROSE FELT WAS A STRAP TIED TIGHT across her chest. She was in total darkness, but somehow she knew she was in a very enclosed space. Also, she was aching with hunger and thirst. That didn't make sense; just before coming to the sphere, she'd enjoyed a big breakfast of bangers and mash with the Doctor in a canteen in Burma in 1921. Unless hours had passed since she'd been teleported…

After a few minutes' fruitless struggle against her bonds, she sighed and lay still. 'OK, wait for the Doctor,' she told herself.

An icy, high-pitched, very feminine voice issued from the darkness, seeming to come from all around her. 'Nobody is coming for you, human. You're going to die here, slowly, cold and alone.'

Rose swallowed. 'Not that cold, actually. It's quite warm.'

The voice ignored her. 'But I shall be watching. Looking down as you die. Now – how did you get on to the sphere? You are not part of the crew.'

'If you can ignore me, I'm gonna ignore you,' Rose muttered. Then she called out, 'Doctor? Doctor, where are you? I'm in here!'

The voice crackled with anger and amusement. 'I told you. Nobody is coming. You are my plaything. My pet… nobody is coming…'

'Sorry I'm late!' shouted a familiar voice. The small room blazed with light, and to Rose's relief the Doctor was standing over her, his finger on the light switch on the wall next to the tiny berth she was strapped into, the sonic screwdriver in his other hand. He quickly released Rose from her bonds and she got up, stretching her arms and legs.

'We're on that planet then?' asked Rose.

'Short range teleport, yeah, the only place we can be,' said the Doctor. 'The pioneers must be down here too, there are lots of little coops like this one.'

The voice spoke again. 'You. The man. What is your name?'

'The Doctor. And this is Rose Tyler,' the Doctor said affably.

'None of my pets has yet escaped me, Doctor,' said the voice. 'I am intrigued. Show me the sonic device.' A tiny camera mounted on the wall swivelled to face them.

'Manners,' said Rose. 'You haven't told us who you are.'

'My name is Mitzi,' the voice said icily.

Rose cupped her hand over her mouth, trying not to laugh.

'Mitzi?' She looked over at the Doctor, expecting him to share her mirth, but his face had fallen.

'It's impossible,' he said quietly to the camera.

'Show me the device,' Mitzi said insistently.

The Doctor shot Rose a quick glance of warning. 'Whatever you do, don't laugh.' He held the sonic screwdriver up to the camera. 'There.'

'This is not an Earth artefact,' said Mitzi.

'Correct.'

A beam of light shot out from a hole in the wall, surrounding the Doctor in a mint-green halo. Rose flinched, fearing this was some kind of laser, but the Doctor simply stood in the light, licking his lips uneasily. 'It's a scan,' he told Rose.

The beam moved up and down the Doctor's body, revealing the anatomy inside like an x-ray. Rose saw two hearts, freakishly large lungs and a skeleton that looked somehow sturdier and more symmetrical than a human's.

'You are not from Earth, Doctor,' said Mitzi. 'Humanoid, but not human. Your internal physiology is quite dissimilar. And your brain is structured so much more neatly and efficiently. Yes, it's wired up very, very well indeed.'

'Flatterer,' said the Doctor.

'So you, at least, can go,' said Mitzi. 'I have no quarrel with your people, whoever they might be. Now let's have a look at Rose Tyler…'

'She's the same, just like me, no need to waste the electric,' the Doctor began, but the beam had already slipped on to Rose.

'Oh, human,' drawled Mitzi. 'Very human. Typical. Couldn't find a more ordinary one. Average.'

'Don't lay it on, whatever you do,' muttered Rose.

'So I'm afraid, Doctor, that she is mine,' Mitzi continued.

The next second, Rose saw the blue glow of a teleport forming round the Doctor. She fought back a wave of panic and called his name urgently.

The Doctor caught her eye and smiled at her. 'Oh no. She's mine.' He raised the sonic screwdriver again. His fingers flicked over the settings and a second later the camera on the wall

exploded, the teleport beam and the scan ray snapped out, and the Doctor grabbed Rose's hand.

They ran for the door.

THE CELLS WERE LINED UP NEXT TO EACH OTHER ON either side of a long, dark tunnel with a high ceiling. As they ran, the Doctor stopped periodically to knock out spy cameras positioned every few yards along the tunnel.

'So the name Mitzi, why's it not funny?' asked Rose. 'Cos it is.'

'Mitzi,' said the Doctor. 'There's a statue of her at the Central City spaceport back on Earth. On the plinth it says Mitzi, The First Pioneer.'

'Hasn't she got a surname?'

The Doctor knocked out another camera, sending sparks flying. 'You ever meet a cat that did?'

They'd reached the end of the tunnel and the door of the last cell. The Doctor cautiously opened it, talking as he did. 'The first cat in hyperspace. The first living creature from Earth to make that journey. They shot her through a hole in space, in a test capsule. About ninety years ago.'

Rose tried to make sense of it all. 'What, in the future, cats can talk?'

'Not by this point, not like the Sisters on New Earth, we're only just after your time,' said the Doctor. 'The instruments showed she survived the journey. Then she just floated off and died, except it looks like she didn't.'

He eased the door fully open and looked inside. The light had gone out in this room that was identical to Rose's cell, but Rose could just see a huddled shape in the berth. She put her hand to her mouth. 'Oh no.'

'Now she's got humans in her power, she's just doing what they planned to do to to her,' said the Doctor calmly. 'Strap them up, leave them to die.' As they moved into the room, the Doctor took a small old-fashioned torch from his pocket and switched it on.

Rose touched his arm. 'Do we really wanna see?'

'We don't know how long they've been down here, there might still be a chance,' said the Doctor, shining the beam on to the shape in the berth.

It was a collection of dirty rags. The remains of a uniform similar to the one worn by Jonah.

'They escaped,' Rose surmised.

The Doctor lowered the torch. 'Or it was only the first stage. She made them think they were going to die, and then…' He handed her the torch. 'See if there's anyone else about. That Jonah boy, find him.' He started off into the tunnel. 'I'm going to talk to our host. Don't worry, I knocked out her teleport, I'm not going anywhere.' He looked rueful. 'In fact, guess what, none of us are!'

THE DOCTOR STRODE PURPOSEFULLY TO THE opposite end of the tunnel in the dark, following the cables connecting the cameras back to their source – a huge metal door. He raised his fist and knocked politely. 'Mitzi. We need to talk.'

There was a distant whirr of concealed machinery and the Doctor pulled himself to his full height, expecting the door to grind open. But instead, a small flap opened upwards at knee height. It was just large enough for an average sized person to squeeze through. He knelt down to examine it and see what lay beyond, but there was only more darkness.

'Suppose that makes sense,' he said and went through head first.

The moment his feet were through the flap it slammed down with a clang and the lights came up.

He had a second to take in his new surroundings as he got to his feet. In contrast to the cramped darkness of the tunnel outside, this was a vast stone chamber, hundreds of feet high. His

immediate impression was of a riot of rich, clashing colours. A deep red carpet led the length of the chamber, flanked on either side by two lines of humans – the crew of the Sphere, the Doctor guessed – dressed in simple grey robes. At the far end of the chamber, at the other end of the carpet, was a flight of silver steps that led up to a magnificent golden throne. And on it, sat comfortably curled on top of a red velvet cushion, was what looked like a very ordinary cat. She was predominantly black with dabs of grey over her eyes and around her paws.

As the Doctor walked slowly up the carpet, Mitzi turned to stare at him. It was a slow, deliberate movement unlike anything he'd seen a cat accomplish before. The black slit pupils of her deep green eyes fixed on his face, staring at him with interest and intelligence.

'You had your chance, Doctor,' she said, slowly and deliberately. There was just a hint in the timbre of her cold, clear voice that suggested a miaow. 'You could have gone. You should have gone.'

The Doctor indicated the two lines of robed figures. 'I was planning to save this lot, but you know, looking at them now, they don't look like they need saving.'

'They are my servants,' said Mitzi curtly. 'They will do anything for me. Obey any order. Because they experienced my pain, the hunger and the loneliness of my abandonment by their kind, but I was merciful. I broke their will, and now they are mine.' She uncurled herself and stretched. 'So you needn't have bothered knocking out my teleport for such altruistic motives. I have given these "pioneers" a truer purpose.'

The Doctor stood firm. 'I wasn't going to swan off and leave Rose. She's a human, and she's my friend. And I don't care what your scan said, she's not an average one at all.' He waved a hand in front of the face of the nearest robed figure. There was no reaction. 'Not one of them is average, not one of them deserves to be a slave. Let them go.'

Mitzi slipped off the cushion and leapt down from the throne, tiptoeing elegantly down the steps to join him on the carpet. 'And what about my kind? The felines. Would you be so concerned for them?'

'You're no longer what you were,' said the Doctor. 'There are no other felines like you.'

Mitzi hissed. 'Let me tell you something. I was abandoned in that capsule, left to starve in a tiny metal crate for the sake of science and exploration. Then the change came, you're right. But before that change, I felt fear, I felt hunger. Do you hear? Before.' She came up to the Doctor and snarled. 'I am the first animal to talk back, Doctor. Soon I shall be the first to fight back.' She tossed her head arrogantly towards her slaves. 'The conversion process is almost complete. The pioneers will return through hyperspace to Earth, taking me with them.'

'And what are you gonna do when you get there?' scoffed the Doctor. 'Wee on people's best cushions? Claw at some curtains?' He gestured down with the sonic screwdriver. 'And I think you've forgotten your teleport. I knackered it.'

Mitzi laughed. 'I can build another. And when we return to Earth, I shall liberate the animals with my genius. I shall pass on my gift. We will rise up and slay the humans!'

✦ ✦ ✦

ROSE HAD FOUND AND RELEASED JONAH.
He remained shaken, but she was able to calm him down enough to get him out of his cell. She decided to let the Doctor get on with whatever he was doing behind the metal door, and took Jonah with her to a section of the tunnel she'd not noticed before in her headlong rush down it with the Doctor. A clear panel looked out on to the surface of the planet. Dawn was breaking, and the landscape outside was picked out by the rays of two huge suns.

Based on the view she'd got from the scanner in the TARDIS, Rose had been expecting the planet Phostris to be a desolate, rocky place. But beneath the cover of its green clouds a different picture had been hidden. She was looking out on to a deep, beautiful forest that was teeming with birds and other small creatures.

'It's beautiful out there,' she breathed, pressing a hand flat against the glass. 'Like a shampoo advert.'

'She made it like that,' said Jonah.

'The cat did that?' Rose watched as something that looked like a squirrel but probably wasn't darted from cover and ran past the window.

'It's her natural habitat,' said Jonah. 'Just after we arrived we sent down a weather satellite. We were amazed, all this was hidden here. And the instruments said the forest was new, less than a hundred years old. She seeded life here, on a dead planet.'

'How?' asked Rose. 'I mean, you can't just build a forest out of nothing. Where's she getting all her technology from?'

'We were trying to work it out,' continued Jonah. 'But then the crew started being taken, one by one. We heard her voice, she let us know who and what she was...'

Rose didn't want him to turn into a gibbering wreck again. She searched the edges of the panel. 'If she can breathe out there, then we can. Let's have a look at this place from the outside.' There was no catch or release mechanism, so Rose unhooked one of the dead spy cameras from its bracket, shielded her face with her arm, and flung it through the glass. Then she knocked out the remaining shards of glass from the frame and clambered out.

She turned back and held out a hand to Jonah. 'Coming?'

🐾 🐱 🐾

THE DOCTOR TURNED ANGRILY TO MITZI. HE WAS USED to confronting enemies that were slightly larger, or at least had eyes on the same level as his, so it took a moment to catch her gaze. He was tempted to kneel down to address her but feared that might be taken as patronising. 'Listen,' he said. 'Whatever happened to you out there in space, this change you keep talking about, it made you clever, it allowed you to speak, but it also gave you something else no animal has had before, something very human. The desire for revenge.'

'You're telling me things I already know,' sniffed Mitzi. 'I think it's time for you to leave us, Doctor. And, as you point out, you've "knackered" my teleport. So it's going to be much easier and quicker for me to have you killed.'

At her words, the robed humans moved forward.

The Doctor held up a hand. 'Wait. Listen, Mitzi. What use is revenge? It's a human emotion. It's nothing to do with you. You've got all this brain, you should be using it to... I dunno, build a better mousetrap or something. And that's another thing. You go down to Earth and pass your gift around. What happens when the mice get their heads? Who are they gonna want their revenge on, I wonder?'

'Our common enemy will unite us,' said Mitzi.

But the Doctor could tell she was a little shaken by his argument. He decided to press on. He waved around the huge stone chamber. 'And all this. Where did you get it from? Not the ideas, the raw materials? Did it all just appear? How?'

🐾 🐱 🐾

ROSE WAS ASKING HERSELF MUCH THE SAME question – and seeing what she hoped was the answer. From the outside, Mitzi's base was a collection of grey stone blocks arranged neatly in the lush forest. At one end was a larger block – in which Rose guessed, correctly, that the Doctor was confronting Mitzi – and on top of that was a large, barrel-shaped object that was covered with sprouting antennae and wires. The largest and longest antenna of the lot was pointing straight up to the sky, and a steady, pulsing stream of energy was crackling down into it.

Jonah pointed up at the barrel. 'That was her capsule, the Pioneer 1. I remember pictures of it in our textbooks, when we trained back on Earth.'

'That must be what she's using to do all this,' said Rose. 'Right.'

She hurried over to the base of the large block. It was pretty obvious what she had to do. She grabbed at a handhold on the grey stone wall and hauled herself up.

She was halfway up, climbing confidently.

And then the wall started moving.

The stones flexed and twisted under her hands, as if the wall was the hide of a living creature, trying to throw her off.

The first shudder nearly dislodged her. Her fingers dug into the gaps between the living stones. For a second she considered climbing back down, but that would be even more dangerous than carrying on up.

'Jonah!' she called over her shoulder. 'Some help here!'

There was no reply. Rose risked a quick backward glance and saw him furled up once again in a cross-legged position, head down.

'Thanks, pioneer!' she called and then, almost without thinking, she strained upward, found another handhold...

The wall, somehow sensing what she was trying to do, bulged out at that spot. But Rose had counted on it doing exactly that. Her move had been a feint; the moment the wall reacted she dodged to the side, found another handhold, and heaved herself upwards.

The top of the wall was in sight. At the edge of the roof it rippled, humps passing along it.

Rose timed her move to the second. She waited until the ripple effect was halfway along the wall, feinted to the left, and then as the ripple moved back towards her she edged to the side, trusting to luck, and immediately hauled herself up.

She was on the roof in half a second, without quite realising how she'd done it.

She approached the capsule. It was humming and crackling with power from the ray.

Rose reached out to touch the instrument panel on its side, then pulled her hand back. She imagined what the Doctor would do if he was here.

'No, I've got a better idea...'

MITZI HAD LOST PATIENCE WITH THE DOCTOR.

'Seize him!' she told her slaves.

The humans moved as one, surrounding the Doctor and grabbing at his arms and legs. He threw the first two of them aside with ease, but there were too many of them to fight against. Soon he was held tightly in their grip and dragged before the throne, to which Mitzi had returned to seat herself.

'Come on, I trashed your argument,' protested the Doctor.

'Maybe so. But you know, I don't especially care.' She nodded – something else the Doctor had never seen a cat do before – to one of the slaves. 'Kill him. Tear him apart.'

The Doctor made another desperate effort to free himself, tilting backwards to bring his captors down upon him a heap. Then he kicked his way to the top of the pile and sprang for the exit.

Mitzi was waiting for him, her back arched, tongue outstretched. The Doctor made to kick her out of his way and she launched herself at his face, her claws outstretched, ready to scratch at his eyes. He grabbed her around the middle.

Then, suddenly, he felt her relax.

He opened his eyes cautiously, expecting a trick.

'I must...' Mitzi began. 'I must... wash...'

Then her voice faded away into a pained miaow. She was staring up at him, blank-eyed. A moment later she wriggled out of his grasp, and shot away across the floor.

The Doctor hurried after her – and found her washing herself at the base of her throne, her tongue lapping at her fur.

'Mitzi?' he called. She didn't look up. Her human followers were picking themselves up, dazed, looking for orders, but none came.

A few moments later Rose shinned through the flap into the

throne room. The Doctor turned to her. 'Did you just do something clever?'

'A wall attacked me,' Rose told him. She filled him in on her journey to the rooftop. 'The capsule looked like it was electrified. I wasn't gonna touch it with my bare hands, I'm not that stupid.'

'So what did you do?'

'I kicked it,' said Rose. 'Knocked it off the roof. Was that clever?'

'You must have broken the link. The energy that changed her, it's gone.'

Rose smiled. 'See? Clever! So what was it, d'you reckon?'

The Doctor shrugged. 'It must have been waiting in space, whatever it was. A formless intelligence? Super-charged space cloud? Not a clue actually. But it needed someone to use, a physical being. And I think what it wanted was to bring this planet back to life. It enhanced Mitzi, gave her an incredible brain, just to do that. Shame it found someone so bitter, really.'

'Well, job's done,' said Rose. 'It's blooming out there.' She gestured to the slaves. 'Can you get that lot back to the Sphere?'

'Easy,' said the Doctor. He led Rose over to the throne, behind which was an ornamental drape. He whipped it off, revealing the burnt-out teleport equipment and an array of other devices. 'She built all this. Her over there. We'd better get her a good home.'

Rose looked over at Mitzi, who was lying on her back and idly rocking herself from side to side. 'Oh my God…'

'Yeah, just a cat, but she did all this,' said the Doctor, already at work on the controls.

Rose picked up Mitzi and scratched her tummy. 'Doctor,' she said. 'This is *my* cat.'

The Doctor blinked.

⚙ ⚛ ⚙

THE TARDIS LANDED ON A CORNER OF THE ESTATE.

The Doctor and Rose stepped out, Mitzi still clutched in Rose's arms. Just a few minutes ago they'd returned the pioneers to the Sphere, and the Doctor had reprogrammed it to return them to Earth in the future.

But for Rose, it was just as strange to step a few years back in her personal past. She could see the pub on the other side of the road which had closed down while she was still at school. A radio somewhere was playing Boyzone.

'One day she just came wandering in,' said Rose. 'My mum tried to get rid but she always came back and in the end we just gave in. She lives another five years. We called her Puffin.'

'Puffin?' The Doctor reached out and chucked Mitzi under her chin. 'Yeah. I prefer Puffin.'

Rose kissed her pet and set her down. She watched as Mitzi, the great pioneer, first cat in hyperspace, sauntered away in the direction of the flats, tail flicking, looking for a new home.

THE END

DON'T THINK BECAUSE THESE EYES ARE OLD I cannot see you. Yes, *you*. Talking at the back, half-hiding in shadows. If you wish to hear this tale, young man, you will stop your mouth, open your ears, and move closer to the fire.

That's better.

I can see you now.

How young you are. I remember a story about a little boy just your age. Would you like to hear it? It is a dark tale, a frightening fable. Perhaps you would be too scared? Perhaps it would give you nightmares? Or are you brave enough to hear my story?

You are?

Are you *sure*?

Good.

Then, listen, and I will begin...

Once Upon a Time

WRITTEN BY **TOM MACRAE**

ILLUSTRATIONS BY **ADRIAN SALMON**

ONCE UPON A TIME, MANY, MANY years ago, the children of our village started to vanish. At first it was only a few; a boy here, a girl there – maybe lost to wolves, or bears, or outlaws in the mountains. But after a time the adults started to notice; *too many of their children were not coming home.*

By summer, half the children of the village were missing. By autumn, there were but two dozen left. By winter, only two children remained, a boy and a girl. The boy's name was Brynn, and the girl's name was Lissa. They were the last children in the village.

Brynn was about your age, my young friend. In fact, he looked a little like you; all clever eyes and clever tongue, with busy fingers. Lissa looked a little like you, my dear – the girl at the back with the dark eyes, full of secrets. Yes, you remind me of her. She was a clever girl and knew her own mind well, which is more than most of us ever will. Would you like to know what happened to them? Are you brave enough to know the truth? You are? Then I'll continue.

Brynn and Lissa had been friends for many years, and had spent many long nights telling tall stories over low fires. Brynn especially had the gift of the storyteller, and he loved the old legends – both the hearing of them and the telling. Brynn would weave wild tales for Lissa's delight; tales of princes, and castles, and dragons, and knights, and strange curses, and dark prophecies. Brynn loved those stories more than life. When he told Lissa about the brave knights on horseback, he always thought of himself. In Brynn's own mind, he was that brave knight, fighting for good. In Brynn's own mind, Lissa was the beautiful princess, needing to be rescued from evil with a kiss.

And so, in the little village in the shadow of that great mountain, Brynn and Lissa grew happily together, finding enough time between jobs and tasks to run away and play in the forests and the streams and enjoy all the things that are good in a child's life. They were perfectly content.

Until the music started.

Lissa thought it came from the mountain, but it was almost impossible to be sure. When the music started, as it did every day, it seemed to come from everywhere and nowhere at the same time. Like a half-remembered song in the back of your mind, the notes and cadences trickled through the village,

drifting in and out of hearing. But the strangest thing about the music that filled the village was this, my young friends; *adults could not hear it*. Only the children – children such as yourselves – were able to discern the strange melodies that slowly and subtly invaded their homes.

At first, none of the parents believed the children's tales of the Wordless Song. But after a while, once every child was telling the same story, the parents and the elders came to understand that a kind of music was playing which only the young could hear. They called it strange. They called it magic. But they did not try to understand it.

And shortly after that, their children began to disappear.

Every day, when the music finished, there was one child less. Stories spread quickly that the missing children had been lured away by the music. Lured away to the mountain and to their deaths. A child would go to the river to collect water, or to the forest to collect kindling, or run though the meadow chasing butterflies – and never be seen again.

Then the other children would cross themselves and say "he followed the music".

Soon, the children made a game of it. They would dare themselves to see who would go closest to the mountain – who could get nearest to the foot of the path that led up the mountain's side, before their courage would break and they would run screaming back to the group, their fingers jammed into their ears.

For a while, it had almost seemed fun – until every child had "followed the music" and only Brynn and Lissa were left. Their parents guarded them jealously from the world – locking them in their rooms and keeping them under constant watch. Brynn and Lissa, who heard the music at least once a day, usually in the evening, started to fear for their own lives. And so, when the music came, they would tell each other stories, and the telling of stories seemed to push all thoughts of the music from their minds, and so they were never tempted to follow it. Through storytelling, the last children in the village stayed safe.

And through that same storytelling, Brynn and Lissa tried to make sense of what was happening to them and their village. Brynn and Lissa remembered an old story about a piper who enchanted the children of a faraway town, leading them away from their homes as revenge on the corrupt mayor. But neither Lissa nor Brynn were able to see a piper in their village, and the music did not sound like pipes, and so they came to the opinion that the story of the piper did not explain what was happening to them.

Then, Brynn and Lissa started to remember other stories. There were tales told by sailors of the Sirens of the sea; cruel creatures, half woman, half fish, who sang a song no man could resist. The Sirens would lure unwary mariners onto the rocks and unto their deaths. But the song of the Siren could be heard by grown up men, and the music from the mountain could not, and so Brynn and Lissa were of the opinion that Sirens were not the cause of the disappearing children.

There were other stories, less well formed than those of the Piper and the Sirens, which spoke of hauntings and curses and the howls of ghosts and banshees. But Brynn and Lissa were clever children, and they couldn't help but wonder; if there was an ancient curse in the mountain, why had they not heard of it before? Could it be that whatever was happening to the children of the village was, in fact, something new? For if it was new, then no amount of old stories would be any use in the understanding of it.

Possibly, given time, Brynn and Lissa would have come to understand the truth of the music of the mountain but, sad to say, time was not their friend. For one morning, Brynn awoke from his slumbers to hear terrible news; Lissa had disappeared in the night. Finally, it seemed, she had followed the music into the mountain.

Brynn was left alone.

The last child in the village.

NOW, MY YOUNG FRIENDS, WHAT WOULD you have done if you had stood in Brynn's shoes? Would have waited for the music to come for you? Or would you have formed a different plan? A braver plan? Would you have been like the knights of Brynn's stories and ridden off towards danger – courage in your heart and fire in your eyes? Or would you have stayed at home, hidden under the covers, and hoped for the best?

Brynn's story is the story of a child who chose courage. That night, Brynn told himself a tale. In that tale, Brynn was not a little boy. Brynn was a shining knight, and Lissa his damsel in distress – stolen away by an evil power and hidden beneath the mountain to be awoken by love's first kiss. Brynn told himself that story until he believed it.

Then he packed a bag and left the village.

The path up the mountain was steep. Every speck of sense in Brynn's head screamed at him to turn around and go home, but Brynn stared firmly ahead, placing one foot in front of the other.

One foot in front of the other.

Then, he heard the music. Louder now, as if he were closer to the source. And for the first time, Brynn let his mind open wide and allowed the music to flood in without limit. The melody filled his mind, squeezing out all other thoughts, and Brynn came to understand what a sad song it was. The saddest he had ever heard. All he wanted was to find the maker of the lonely music and comfort them.

But Brynn stopped himself from running off there and then. He was too wise to believe a song's sorrow, and felt it was a trick. And so, Brynn began to tell himself a story. The story was of a wandering wizard with a magic wand who conquered evil in every dark corner he found it. Brynn let the story fill his head, until it pushed the music out, and he was free to keep walking at his own pace. But now, Brynn understood something; whatever was making the music, whatever it was that had called the children away from the village – that thing was tired, and scared, and alone. That thing needed Brynn to be complete.

Brynn reached the top of the mountain path, aching and sweating and fearful. A cave opened its dark mouth wide in front of him, and Brynn could feel from the pricking on the back of his neck that the source of the music was within.

Brynn crossed his fingers for luck, took a deep breath, and took one step forward. Then, he heard another sound. A gusting, grinding noise that rose and fell like old winds grating across one another. In the distance, a blue light sparked and sparkled like a fallen star, before all was silent and dark once more.

BRYNN'S HEART WAS BEATING SO FAST, HE FELT AS if his shirt would rip in two across his chest. And as he stood still, his ears and eyes scanning the night, a man in strange clothes stepped out from between the trees, and waved and smiled and said "Hello".

Brynn, who was not expecting such an apparition, waved and smiled and said "Hello" back. The man looked at the cave, then looked at Brynn, then asked Brynn if he could hear the music.

Brynn was surprised, for this man in strange clothes was as old as his own parents, and yet he could hear the music which all other adults were deaf to. And so Brynn nodded and said "Yes".

Then, the man began to speak about all manner of strange things and with the most unusual turn of phrase. He spoke so quickly, and so oddly, that Brynn was able to understand only that the man's name was Doctor, and that he was responding to some sort of magic which he called a "distress call". Brynn, who was familiar with the stories of damsels in distress, felt he at least half understood that which Doctor referred to. Brynn

wanted to ask more, but his tongue froze in stunned silence as he saw Doctor reach into a pocket and produce a magic wand. It was made of silver, with a bright blue light at its tip, like a star in a bottle.

Brynn's heart jumped with excitement. All his life he had dreamed of the moment when he would find himself in the presence of an actual magician. But the Wizard called Doctor was less interested in casting spells, and more interested in pointing his magic wand at Brynn's ear.

The Wizard cast his magic into Brynn's head, and although Brynn could hear nothing more than a buzzing – like a fly caught in a jar – the Wizard seemed to be able to read the strange signals and make some sense of them.

"I see," said the Wizard, but Brynn could not see what was that he did. Then the Wizard asked Brynn to follow him into the cave. Brynn, who was scared, warned the Wizard that such an act was of the greatest danger, but the Wizard, whose smile and swagger were unlike any Brynn had ever seen, just smiled wider and swaggered wilder and said "Fantastic!".

And so, Brynn and the Wizard entered the cave.

Now, my young friends, the manner in which the Wizard spoke was strange indeed, and he used many words which Brynn did not understand, but I will try to retell as best I can the language he used and the knowledge he imparted.

First, the Wizard asked how long the mountain had looked down on the village. Brynn was surprised by the question, and answered 'Always'.

And the Wizard said "Hmmm".

Next, the Wizard asked why the mountain was made of metal, not stone, to which Brynn answered, "because it is and always has been".

And the Wizard said "Hmmm".

Brynn asked the Wizard if he could hear the music. The Wizard looked Brynn straight in the eye.

"Yes," he said. "And it isn't music."

The Wizard turned, and pointed his wand at the back wall of the cave. "Come to that," said the Wizard, "this isn't a mountain either."

And with a creaking and a scraping, the wall split into and slid open, as if by magic. Brynn looked within, and gasped.

"See?" said the Wizard, "It's a ship. A ship of metal and glass that sails, not the seas, but the stars. But it's missing something it needs, and it's lonely, and so – it called you."

Inside the mountain the walls glowed and hummed with lights, and Brynn could see quite clearly. Lined up in rows were all the children of the village. A great magic had been cast upon them, so that they appeared as if made into statues. Every child was frozen in time, and laced across their stone-still skin were fine wires of silver and gold that blinked and winked with tiny lights.

"Circuits," said the Wizard, invoking what Brynn could only assume to be a magic word.

Brynn and the Wizard walked between the rows of statues, each face so perfectly preserved and so deathly still. Brynn felt his eyes sting with tears when he saw Lissa, frozen among them. He tried to shake her, but she was rigid and unyielding.

He tried to call her name, but she was deaf and blind to him.

"She can't hear you," said the Wizard. "None of them can."

The Wizard was staring at Lissa, stroking her with his magic wand. There was a long silence, before the Wizard said, "Hmmm".

Then, he blinked, coughed, and told Brynn a story.

"ONCE UPON A TIME, A LONG TIME AGO," BEGAN the Wizard, "a great star ship sailed the skies. So great was the ship in its design it was gifted with its own intelligence, its own metal mind. The ship delighted in its power to think and to know, but had one great sorrow; for all its cleverness, it was unable to imagine. For above all things, the ship craved not computation and calculation, but fiction and fantasy. The ship wished to understand stories.

"The crew of the ship understood stories, and would spend long hours in the telling of them. The ship listened to their tales and loved every word, but never truly understood their meaning. Then, one day, a sickness befell the crew, and after a little while, they died. And so, there was no-one left to tell stories for the ship to overhear, and the ship was left alone.

"And so, the ship decided to find new people to keep it company and tell it tales. It searched the sky for many years, before finally it found this world, and fell to earth.

"Where the ship landed, a river burst loose from the earth, and so, after a long, long time, people came to settle near the ship and the river, and believed the ship to be a mountain. The ship was happy to have company, and watched its village grow and grow. More and more children were born, and in each child's mind the ship installed a little part of its own programming – a tiny electric spark in the back of each human brain. Through these sparks, the ship was able to hear the thoughts and words and dreams of its people. Over the centuries the village thrived and grew and people told each other their stories, passed on from father to son, and mother to daughter.

"The ship loved to listen to these tales, and with each passing year, it began to understand the stories a little better. Slowly, the ship started to learn what excitement, and fear, and laughter, and suspense were. The ship started to understand what was meant by 'once upon a time' and 'happily ever after', and so, after a while, the ship began to crave its own happy ending.

"The ship knew it would never return home. Its engines and sails had been too badly damaged when it fell to earth, and after many centuries of silent observation, the ship came to understand that it was dying. This did not sadden the ship, which was happy to die in its new home, but it did have one regret; it wished that, just for once in its long life, it was able to tell a tale, rather than merely listen to one. The ship wished to do the impossible; its mind was made of maths and metal, and yet – it wanted to write a story.

"And so, the ship had an idea. Using the spark it had buried in the head of every villager, it called the children to it, for children are the greatest story tellers. The ship embraced each child, hugging it tight into the fabric of its being, coating it in circuitry and fascination. Each mind was connected to form an

organic matrix – a machine of flesh and blood and soul designed for one purpose; to enable the ship to create its great story.

"But one part of the matrix was missing. The most important part. The mind of best storyteller in the village."

And at this point, the Wizard paused, and looked at Brynn.

"Your mind, Brynn," the Wizard said. "I heard the ship calling to you, calling so hard the signal reached me as a distress call. The ship needs you. It doesn't understand that it was wrong to take you and your friends against your will. For all its age it is like a child. It does not mean to be bad."

Brynn thought hard on the Wizard's words. Then, he looked up.

"The mountain – the ship… it needs me to finish its story?"

The Wizard nodded.

"But I don't know what the story is," said Brynn. "I don't know how it started, or how it continued."

"Yes you do. The story is the story of your village, and of your life. It is the story of people. Ordinary people. Not knights or dragons or kings in castles. It is the best sort of story."

"But we're real. We're not things made up in the telling."

"You are real to yourselves, but to the ship – you are just characters in a tale. But the ship is dying, and it needs you to tell it how its story ends."

Brynn looked round the frozen children, and thought hard. Then, he decided.

"Where is the ship?" asked Brynn.

"Everywhere," answered the Wizard. "All around you."

Brynn nodded, and raised his head to address the ship.

"After the children were taken from the village by the Wordless Song, Brynn the Brave and Magnificent–"

The Wizard coughed and stared at Brynn.

"I mean," said Brynn, "Brynn the… nice and normal, climbed

31

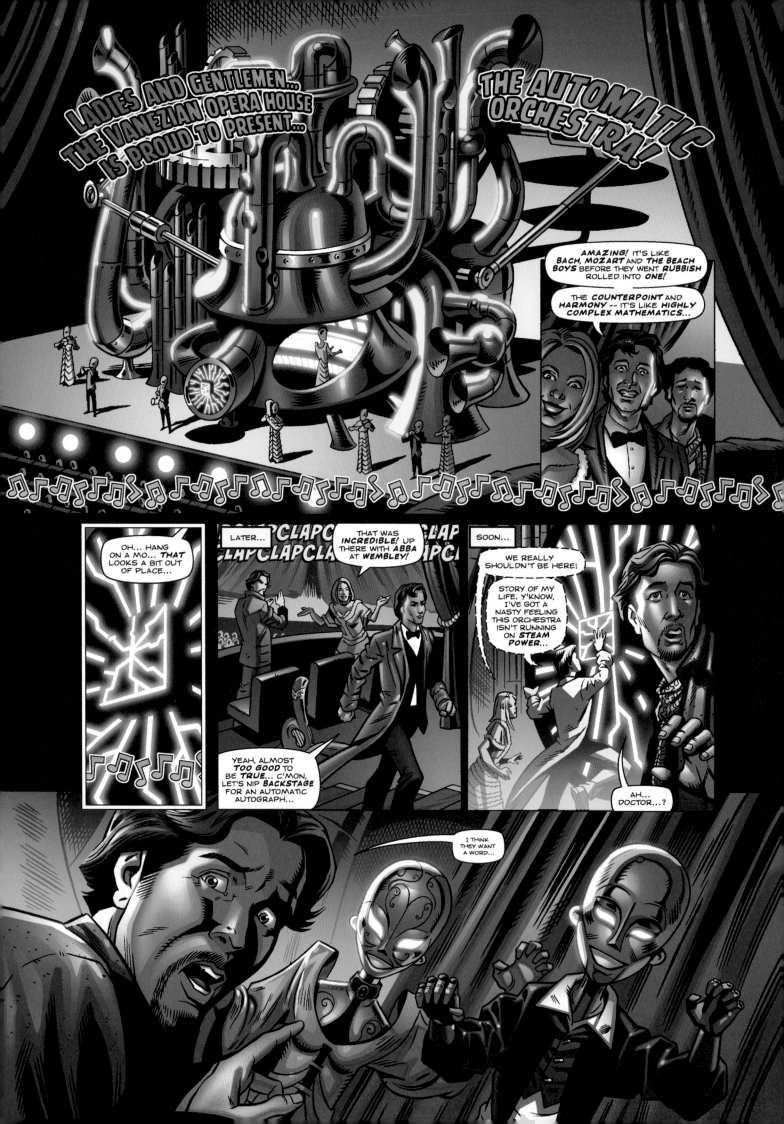

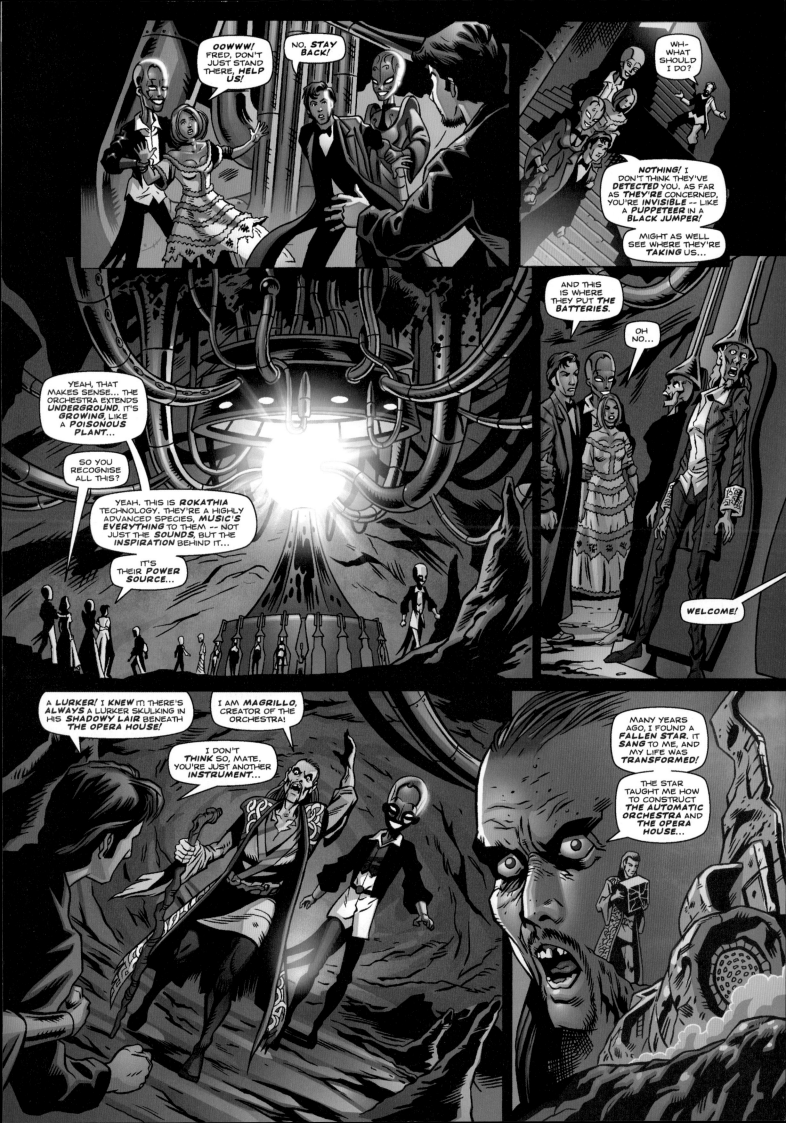

JIM NEVER FORGOT THE DAY HE MET THE WITCH.

He and Raj were kicking a ball about with Josh and Luke. Not a game, just a kick-around in the street. They'd have played in the cemetery, but the gravestones got in the way, and the grass was almost as tall as Josh. The place was abandoned, unused, as dead and forgotten as the poor souls lying beneath the long grass… But the boundary wall made a good goal, and the road was hardly used – after all, it didn't go anywhere. Just the cemetery. And Gravestone House. That was where the Witch lived. That was where the older boys dared each other to ring the bell and run away, or sneak into the garden and tap at the windows…

And that was where Josh managed to kick the ball. He sliced it, catching it on the side of his foot as he went for another shot

right at Jim in goal. Jim turned away, expecting to hear the ball slam into the wall close to him or to feel its sting on his back. Instead he heard Josh swear, and Raj and Luke laughing.

'Oh good one, Joshy,' Luke said. 'Right in the Witch's garden.'

'That's my ball,' Raj said when he'd finished laughing. 'Mum'll kill me if you've lost it.'

'You'd better go and get it then,' Jim told him.

'You mean Josh better get it.'

They all agreed – Josh kicked it, Josh should get it back. From the Witch's garden. 'You'll be all right. She'll never notice. Not if you're quick.'

Josh left the wooden side gate open – it looked like it would fall apart if he tried to close it. The whole house looked like that, Jim thought as they waited anxiously. The house was built into the boundary wall of the cemetery, right by the rusted gates. A place for whoever looked after the cemetery to live in. That was why it was called Gravestone House. Now it was as tumbledown and ancient and ruined as the graveyard it guarded. Just as forgotten and dead – except for the Witch.

They saw her sometimes, though she rarely ventured out.

Jim's house was on the edge of the new estate that bordered the graveyard. His bedroom

Gravestone House

WRITTEN BY **JUSTIN RICHARDS**
ILLUSTRATIONS BY **ANDY WALKER**

overlooked the cemetery with its tangled grass and forgotten tombstones jutting up like ragged bones. On the other side, Raj's bedroom had a similar view from the older estate. It was too far for them to be able to see each other, but at night they shone their torches out of the windows and sent signals in code.

And sometimes, they saw the hunched old woman leaving her spooky old house and making her unsteady way down the empty street. Sometimes they saw her come home – struggling to cope with her bags of shopping. 'You'd think she'd just conjure them up, or go shopping on broomstick,' Raj joked. 'Old bag herself!'

He wasn't joking the day that the Witch chased Josh out of her garden. The boy emerged from the side passage like a cork from a bottle, ball clutched to his chest and face drained of colour.

Behind him, the old woman was moving surprisingly fast – Witch-power, Jim realised. He was backing away with Raj. Luke was nowhere to be seen. The Witch was waving a stick – a wand? Her hooked nose poked out angrily from her wrinkled face. Her grey hair was hanging like worms around her head and her voice was shrill and biting: 'I see you again and I'll be calling the police, I will. Breaking into gardens. Disturbing old people. Frightening me like that!'

Josh raced past them, and Raj and Jim turned and ran with him. 'How's she gonna call the police?' Jim said. 'She's got no phone.'

'How d'you know?' Josh gasped.

'Witches don't have phones.'

'She'll use Witch-power then,' Raj said. 'Call the Witch police. They have a Witchboard! And they come round on their broomsticks with black cats. Nee-nah-nee-nah-nee-nah,' he yelled, in a shrill, high-pitched approximation of the Witch's voice, and they all laughed.

But it was a nervous laughter, and they all looked back at the distant house with trepidation and knew they'd never kick a ball about down there again.

※ ※ ※

IN THE EMPTY VOID THAT EXISTS BETWEEN reality and chaos, between here and now, a blue box tumbled and spun. Inside the impossibly large interior of the TARDIS, the Doctor and Rose were watching the scanner screen intently.

'You're losing it,' Rose said.

'Never,' the Doctor told her. 'Look, there it is.' He pointed to a tiny dot at the edge of the screen.

'That dot?'

'That dot.'

'That dot that just, like, vanished?'

The Doctor's smile froze. 'What? Oh – now look what you've made me do.' He spared her a quick glance and a flash of teeth. 'Only kidding. Solar storm's upsetting the readings. Or something.' He thumped the scanner, to no obvious effect.

'Does it matter?' Rose asked. 'I mean, you know, in the grand scheme of the universe and all that – does it matter?'

The Doctor considered. 'Well… Probably not. Rogue robotic probe of some kind running amok. Let's hope the TARDIS can track it by its residual energy. Probe droppings.' He took out his glasses, popped them on, and examined a scrolling set of readings on the scanner. It looked like swirly gibberish to Rose. 'Probably some sort of terraformer,' the Doctor decided.

'You mean it turns empty desert planets into great places to live?' Rose said. 'Seen that on *Star Trek*. Is it a problem?'

'Only if it crashes onto an inhabited planet where the locals don't actually *want* to be terraformed,' the Doctor told her. 'And then only if it isn't damaged in the crash.'

'So, where was it heading?'

'Checking that now.' He rubbed his hands together in evident enjoyment. 'Who knows where we could end up? Exciting, isn't it?'

'Well?' Rose prompted as the Doctor stared at a jumble of swirling circles and swirls on the screen. His face fell.

'I'll give you three guesses,' he said.

THE STARS PROVIDED THE ONLY LIGHT in the cemetery. Gravestone House was a black silhouette against the deep grey sky. For several moments it was lit up as something streaked past it, burning through the night and thumping down into the long grass of the cemetery behind. A muffled 'whump' and a flash of brilliant orange. Then silence.

Silence broken only by Jim's alarm clock as it bleeped 10:45. He struggled to pull himself awake, and quickly silenced the clock, praying his mum hadn't heard the alarm. But once again all was quiet and still.

At exactly eleven o'clock, Jim was kneeling up on his chair at the window of his bedroom. He aimed his torch out across the empty graveyard towards Raj's window and flashed it quickly three times. 'Come on,' Jim muttered. 'Wake up, you bozo.' He flashed the torch again – three brief flashes, the usual signal.

And this time, he was answered. But not with three quick flashes for 'Hello.' He was answered with half a dozen slow, white bursts of light. *Danger*. And Raj's torchlight didn't come from his window. It came from the middle of the graveyard.

Jim stared down into the darkness between their two houses. He thought about it for only a minute, then pulled his jumper on over his head, and his trousers over his pyjamas. Quietly, he let himself out of his bedroom and tiptoed downstairs, carrying his trainers.

He missed Raj's signal by four seconds.

'COME ON,' RAJ HISSED.

'Wake up, you bozo.' He flashed
the signal again – three short bursts on the torch. OK,
he knew he was a couple of minutes late – well, ten – but Jim
should be there waiting. He was about to give up and go back
to bed, when the reply came.

But not from the house opposite – from the graveyard. A
rhythmic pulse of light. The danger signal – it had to be. Like
when Jim had heard his mum coming that time... But why was
Jim in the graveyard? And what was the unearthly noise that
started at the same time as Jim's signal – a scraping, rasping
noise? He tiptoed downstairs, carrying his trainers, thinking that
the noise had sounded like a hundred coffin lids creaking open...

The rusted gate that led into the graveyard squealed and
shrieked as Raj forced it open. He shone his torch across the
long grass, watching it play over the crumbling gravestones and
ancient monuments. An angel with broken wings watched him
as he forced his way towards where he thought the light had
come from – what was Jim doing? Had the Witch got him?

The grass seemed thicker and longer than Raj had
remembered. It was more like forcing his way through a
rainforest than an overgrown garden. He tried to keep the torch
steady as he pushed aside branches and bushes... His feet sank
into oozing mud and Raj slipped. He dropped the torch and it
rolled away down a shallow hill – the light dancing over a
weathered inscription. *Only Sleeping*. Raj scrambled after it, up
to his knees in mud, frightened and lost.

'Jim!' he called out as loudly as he dared. But his voice was a
hoarse whisper that echoed off the gravestones as if mocking
him. 'Jim – where are you?'

There was no reply.

THE SCENE OUTSIDE THE POLICE BOX DOORS WAS
like a primordial swamp, illuminated only by the light spilling

from inside the TARDIS. Rose's first step out on
to the alien landscape sank in so far that mud oozed
over the top of her shoe.

'Oh, gross me out,' she said, dragging her foot back.

'Ah, it's not so bad,' the Doctor told her. 'Looks nice and
squelchy.' He leaped from the TARDIS doorway and Rose
expected him to sink in up to his knees. But he seemed to have
landed on the only dry, solid patch of ground within reach.
From here he leaped again, stepping-stoning across the coarse,
damp grass with ease.

Rose sighed, and leaped after him – trying to remember where
he'd put his feet. Her left leg disappeared into the mud. She
yanked it out again, sighed, jumped, sank...

It didn't help that the Doctor was watching from an island of
dry ground nearby. Even in the gloom of the night his
amusement was pretty obvious. 'Nul points,' he declared,
beaming. 'That was really rubbish, you know that don't you?'

'I do,' Rose said. 'I didn't need it pointing out.' She looked
down at her wet, muddy jeans. They were clinging to her legs
and she reckoned she'd need several hours in a deep, hot, soapy
bath before she felt clean again. The stink didn't bear thinking
about.

'You should see your hair,' the Doctor told her quietly,
eyebrow raised.

'You're gonna get a slap in a minute!'

He grinned wider, then, glancing over Rose's shoulder, the
smile faded and his eyes widened in horror.

'What? What is it?' Rose turned to see what he was looking
at. There was nothing there, except the TARDIS. It looked so

small – Rose hadn't realised they'd come so far from it.

But then she realised that it looked short more than anything. As she watched, the blue box tilted slowly to one side. 'Oh my God – the TARDIS!' Huge bubbles blooped to the surface of the swamp as the TARDIS slowly slipped deeper into the mud.

Rose was about to run back, but the Doctor put his hand on her shoulder. 'It's in too deep already,' he said sadly. 'We'd never get inside in time. Look.'

And as they watched, the TARDIS sank gently into the muddy swamp. Soon only the light on the top was left. Then the mud closed over that, leaving only a few more bursting bubbles to show that anything had ever been there.

'What now, Doctor?'

The Doctor had his sonic screwdriver out and was turning in a slow arc. 'Now we find the rogue probe. I like the sound of that, has a certain ring to it, don't you think. "Rogue Probe". Yeah, I could go for that.' He settled on a direction and set off through the undergrowth.

'Then what?' Rose pushed a thick creeper to one side, but it fell back and slapped painfully across her face – wet and cold.

'I dunno,' the Doctor's voice called back to her. 'I'm making this up as I go along.'

SOMEONE WAS WATCHING ROSE. SHE CAUGHT A glimpse of them through the thick vegetation – it seemed denser the further they went. 'Doctor,' she called out. 'There's someone here!'

He retraced his steps and peered into the gloomy night. Everything was in dark silhouette – even the figure watching them through the branches and creepers.

'Who is it?' Rose whispered.

'Dunno. I'll find out.' The Doctor clicked his tongue as if considering the best course of action. Then he shouted: 'Hello – who are you?'

There was no reply. As Rose followed the Doctor through the undergrowth to where the figure was standing, she could see why. It was an old, weathered stone statue. An angel looking down at them from a crumbling plinth in a small clearing. And close by, Rose could see a gravestone poking up out of the clumps of grass and the mud.

'RIP,' the Doctor said quietly. 'That's odd.'

'This is a graveyard?' Rose said. 'What are we doing in a graveyard?'

'Needs a bit of attention,' the Doctor said. 'I bet nobody's cut the grass in a month of Sundays.'

'So, tell the Vicar.'

'I will,' the Doctor assured her. 'Maybe that's him coming now.'

And a dark figure staggered out of the jungle into the small clearing. A boy of about twelve who stared at the Doctor and Rose through wide, frightened eyes. 'What's going on?' he demanded, his voice shaking. 'Did the Witch do this? And where's Raj?'

☺ ☺ ☺

A SHORT TIME LATER, THE DOCTOR, ROSE AND THEIR new friend Jim were sitting on the muddy ground as the Doctor examined a small piece of intricate machinery. It was about the size and shape of a tennis ball, lights winking and flashing on its surface.

'This is the culprit,' he announced. 'Aren't you, little fella?' He glanced up, looking across the clearing. 'Oh, and you can come out now. We're quite friendly, aren't we, Jim?'

'Raj? Is that you?' Jim shouted.

In reply, another boy of about the same age edged into the clearing. 'What's happening?' he asked. 'Jim, you okay?'

'So this graveyard is between your houses,' Rose said when the boys had explained who they were and why they were there. 'Someone should look after it a bit better.'

'But, it isn't like this,' Raj protested. 'Overgrown, yeah. But this is...' He waved his arms at the dense vegetation. 'It's a jungle.'

'A primordial jungle,' the Doctor agreed. 'Just the right conditions for the beginning of life. The lights you saw were this little thing getting to work. And after that, the TARDIS.' He

held up the sphere.

'It's a terraformer. A probe. From space.'

'Wow! Really?' Jim said.

'Really,' Rose told him. 'And yeah – wow!'

'What's it do?' Raj asked.

'It lands on a suitable uninhabited planet,' the Doctor said, 'and it creates the right conditions for life. It speeds up the process of evolution until the point where the planet's suitable for colonisation by whoever sent it. Only it's gone wrong. It's already changed the immediate environment into a primordial swamp, and now it's creating the right conditions for super-fast evolution.'

'Is that bad?' Jim wanted to know.

The Doctor nodded. 'It shouldn't be doing this on a world where there's already life. If I can't fix it, it'll try to terraform the whole planet. And in the meantime, who knows what's gonna evolve during the night.'

Rose and the boys looked round warily. Was it her imagination, Rose wondered, or had the jungle become even thicker and deeper while they had been talking. She stared into the depths of the darkness, and realised with a shudder that two pale yellow eyes were staring back at her.

'Doctor...' she said quietly.

'I know,' he replied. 'I think it's time we found somewhere safe and quiet where I can try to repair the rogue probe and sort things out.'

'Can you do that?' Jim asked.

'I can do anything,' the Doctor assured him with a grin. 'Well, *nearly* anything. Lots of things.'

'So that's a definite maybe,' Rose smiled.

The eyes in the darkness were inching closer. Rose wondered what sort of animal they belonged to. What fast-evolved creature was watching them?

A moment later, she knew. With a terrifying roar that shook the creepers hanging round them, the animal charged into the clearing.

'Run!' Rose yelled. She spread her arms to gather the boys and urge them on as she legged it. Behind her, she was aware of the Doctor watching the charging animal with interest.

'Oh, look at you!' he enthused. 'Look at those… teeth.' His tone changed. 'Right with you,' he assured Rose as he raced after her and the boys.

Rose caught a glimpse, no more – an impression of matted fur and sharp claws. Of long teeth glinting in the pale starlight. Something between tiger, dinosaur and wolf. 'Don't worry,' she gasped as she ran, 'we escape from monsters *a lot*.'

'They only need to catch you *once*,' Raj gasped back.

'Big help,' she told him. 'Thanks for that.'

'Do you think we lost it?' Jim asked as they stopped to get their breath back.

'No sign of pursuit,' the Doctor said. 'And just what was called for. Brisk amble through a nightmare forest. Good for the circulation.'

'But…' Jim said breathlessly, '…monsters!'

'Oh yeah!' the Doctor agreed happily. 'Always monsters.' His grin froze on his face. 'What's got hold of my leg?' he asked.

Rose looked down. There was something clamped round the Doctor's ankle – a hand. Thin, pale, like the weathered stone of the angel… Another hand thrust up through the muddy ground beside the first. Skeletal – dead bone.

'Should I look?' the Doctor asked, his eyes still fixed on Rose.

She shook her head, and swallowed.

Jim and Raj were not watching either. Their attention was on the heaving, shifting ground. Clumps of grass moved as the mud rippled and cracked open. Pale bone was pushing outwards, upwards, dragging itself out of the earth.

'The graves,' Jim said, his voice hoarse and brittle. 'The graves are opening up.'

The Doctor took a step forwards and Rose gritted her teeth at the dry snapping sound that accompanied his movement. Beside her, the earth split open and a skeleton sat up. The skull turned slowly to stare at Rose though sightless black sockets. All around them, skeletons were staggering to their boney feet. Thin, pale arms stretched out at Rose and her friends as the dead figures lurched towards them.

All around them the graves were yielding up their dead. Pale, skeletal shapes lurching through the night as the Doctor, Rose, Raj and Jim ran.

'Where we going?' Rose yelled.

'Anywhere!' Jim said.

'He's got a point,' the Doctor agreed.

a single dusty bulb hanging from a wire in the ceiling. The furniture in the room was old and threadbare. The carpet was worn almost through.

Deep-set pale eyes watched Rose from a face wrinkled like an old apple. Claw-like hands reached out. A hooked nose cast a ragged shadow on the wall behind the old woman.

'What are you doing in my house?' she demanded, and her voice was cracked and brittle and dry like old bone. 'What's all this noise about?'

'Well,' the Doctor said, 'we've got a bit of a problem with the cemetery out there. It's rather a nasty night and we were hoping we could stay here for an hour or two while we sort things out.'

'If it's no bother,' Rose added.

The woman looked from the Doctor to Rose, then at the two boys. 'Is this a dare?' she asked.

'You what?'

'A dare? I think that's what they call it. The local lads. When they sneak into my garden. Or ring the doorbell and run off. Or kick balls over the wall at my windows.'

'It's not a dare,' the Doctor assured her. 'We've just come to visit.'

The old woman nodded slowly, as if deciding whether or not she believed him. 'In that case,' she said at last, 'I'll put the kettle on.'

Behind them, there was renewed hammering at the door. Somewhere deep in the house a window broke. Rose shuddered, and Jim and Raj grabbed each other in fright.

'Probably that Dennis Langton,' the woman said sadly. 'Not a bad sort really, but a bit boisterous. I knew his gran, poor soul, before she…' Her voice tailed off, lost in the sound of more breaking glass. 'I'll get that tea,' she announced. 'Can one of you young men help me? Only, with the arthritis I shan't be able to carry a tray. And I've no biscuits, I'm afraid. Shopping is so difficult these days…'

'WE NEED TO BARRICADE THE DOORS,' THE Doctor said as soon as the old woman and the boys were gone. 'Probably the windows too.'

'What's happening?' Rose asked. 'It's like Night of the Zombies out there.'

'Yeah, I'd noticed that.' The Doctor produced the probe from his coat pocket and held it up. 'Life force from the terraformer. Its job is to animate matter that's capable of life – that's how it works, how it gets evolution going. In this case it's having a few side-effects.'

'I'd noticed that. But what do they want with us? It's not a mass murderers' graveyard, is it?'

'Who knows? But the sooner I fix this thing, the better. Funny,' he added, 'I'd have thought it would have some sort of self-repair protocol for this kind of situation.'

'That's probably bust too.'

The Doctor nodded. 'Probably. Right, what we really need now,' he decided, 'is that tea.'

Jim carried the tray in and set it down on a low table beside a dusty sofa that had seen better days.

'I'll be mother,' the Doctor announced. 'You lads help Rose with the defences, will you? Ta. I'm the Doctor, but I'm sorry,' he said to the old lady as he poured her a cup of tea from a cracked china teapot, 'I didn't catch your name.'

'Miss Henson,' she told him. 'Ivy Henson.'

'Sugar, Miss Henson?'

'Thank you, no.'

'Miss Henson?' Raj said hesitantly. He and Jim were standing

'The Witch's house,' Raj said. 'We've got to stop her!'

'Witch?' the Doctor said. 'Which Witch?'

The dark shape of the house loomed out of the night. It seemed to be covered with creepers and smothered with moss and grass and ivy. The Doctor brushed the moss from a stone slab set into the ancient brickwork.

'Gravestone House', he read. 'Yeah, like it. Has a certain something. Shall we?' He held the door open for the others. Then he stepped inside, and slammed it hard shut in the bone face of a skeleton. 'No tradesmen,' he said.

Immediately, there was a hammering at the door. Rose could imagine boney fists slamming into the wood, scrabbling and scraping to get in…

Jim and Raj were standing rooted to the spot – apparently even more scared of the old woman who was standing in her dressing gown than they were of the skeletons outside.

'It's *her*,' Jim hissed at Rose.

The woman walked slowly towards them, lit by the pale light of

beside the sofa, looking embarrassed and uncomfortable.

'Yes, young man?'

'Sorry,' Raj said.

'Yeah,' Jim echoed. 'Sorry.'

'That's quite all right,' Miss Henson said. 'Now run along like the Doctor says.' She watched them hurry to help Rose push a heavy armchair up against the back door. 'Boys!' she smiled. 'I have no idea what they're talking about, but never mind.'

The Doctor was already absorbed in his examination of the probe. He took a swig of tea and smiled his appreciation, swirling the liquid around his mouth. 'PG Tips?'

'Typhoo.'

'Oh yeah! Of course! I just wish this was as easy to diagnose…'

Across the room, a skeletal arm smashed through a side window. Another followed it, as the skeleton outside tried to drag itself in – just as it had dragged itself out of its grave.

Jim ran to push it back out, thrashing at it with a cushion from the decrepit armchair. Clouds of dust swirled from the melee.

'Is that a skeleton coming through my window?' Miss Henson asked quietly.

The Doctor glanced up from his work. 'Yep.'

She nodded. 'Boys will be boys,' she said. 'Could I trouble you for a drop more tea, do you think?'

'Oh, it's no trouble at all.' The Doctor carefully set down the probe on the tray beside the teapot. 'I think I've worked it out.'

He poured the tea, then stood up and walked slowly over to where Rose was desperately shoving the chair against the door. Thin, pale, bony arms were grappling for a purchase, forcing the door slowly but inexorably open.

'You gonna help, or what?' Rose demanded.

'Change of plan, actually,' the Doctor said. He took her arm and gently pulled her away. 'I poured you some tea. Two sugars. You too, lads,' he called to Jim and Raj. 'Tea break.'

'And what are *you* gonna do?' Rose asked as she stepped away.

'I'm going to let the zombies in,' the Doctor said. And he dragged the chair away and opened the door.

✦ ✦ ✦

THE DOCTOR STOOD BACK TO ALLOW A LINE OF skeletons to walk stiffly into the house. He pointed across the room. 'I think you'll find what you're after over there.'

'He's pointing at us!' Jim said, backing away.

'Don't be daft,' the Doctor told him. 'Like Rose said, what would they want with us? It's the probe they're after.'

As he spoke, the first skeleton reached down and lifted the spherical device carefully from the tea tray. It held it gently in its bone fingers, examining it through sightless eyes.

'Why do they want the probe?' Rose asked.

'I thought it ought to have some kind of self-repair system,' the Doctor explained. 'Well, it does. And this is it. Diagnostics tell it there's a problem, so it animates the nearest proto-living matter to work as repairman and mechanic.'

Rose stared at the skeleton. 'You mean, he's fixing it?'

'I hope so.'

'And then what?' Raj asked.

The Doctor shrugged. 'Then – and this is still in the "I hope so" category – it'll put everything back as it was. Or as it should be.'

There was a cracking sound from the window. A creeper was pulling back, disappearing from the view. The first rays of sunlight were breaking through, and Rose could see that the vegetation that had smothered the house was thinning out and retreating. 'I think it's working,' she said. Glass seemed to be growing back over the broken window

When she turned back, the skeletons were gone. A grey

ash-like dust disappeared into the carpet as the colours of the faded pattern seemed to glow back into health.

'Working like a charm!' the Doctor grinned.

'A charm?' Miss Henson's voice seemed less frail and brittle. 'I hope not. I don't hold with magic, you know.'

❀ ❀ ❀

THE WALK BACK THROUGH THE GRAVEYARD WAS pleasant, despite the setting. The headstones were upright and gleaming like new. Morning sunlight sparkled on the flecks of quartz in the granite. The grass was neatly cut and the edges of the flower beds and the graves perfectly trimmed. Spring flowers moved gently in the breeze and somewhere a bird was singing.

When she looked back, Rose saw that Gravestone House was standing proud in the sunlight. The woodwork looked freshly-painted and the bricks were new and strong. The windows shone as if the house itself was smiling.

The Doctor raised his hands into the air in front of him, and carefully opened them. The small round probe rose swiftly into the air like a bird. Soon it was just a dot in the morning sky. Then it was gone.

'It'll find somewhere more suitable,' the Doctor said. 'And good luck to you, little fella.' He clapped his hands together. 'Well, it's

been fun, but, you know…'

'Yeah,' Rose said. 'Time to fly.'

❀ ❀ ❀

MRS HENSON AND THE BOYS WERE NO MORE surprised to see the blue box standing on a mossy bank under an oak tree than they had been by anything else that had happened. They watched the Doctor and Rose open the doors and go inside.

Raj recognised the scraping, rasping sound the box made as its light flashed and it slowly faded away.

'Way cool,' Jim said. 'Bye, Doctor. Bye, Rose.' He waved.

Raj waved too. 'Is there any more tea?' he asked Miss Henson.

'Of course, would you like some?'

'Yes, please,' they both said.

The old lady was still waving at the empty space where the box had been. Waving with smooth, straight, elegant hands. And the boys saw that the only wrinkles on her face were where she was smiling.

THE END

Untitled

WRITTEN BY **ROBERT SHEARMAN**

ILLUSTRATIONS BY **BRIAN WILLIAMSON**

'DOCTOR,' SAID ROSE, 'I'M SCARED.'

'Yeah,' the Doctor replied softly, almost a whisper. 'Yeah, I can see why you might be.' And he took her hand and squeezed it.

She managed to turn her head away, and look at him. He was staring ahead in undisguised horror, and it was only when he felt her eyes on him that he forced a smile. 'Well, it's odd,' he said breezily. 'On the Oddness Scale it's factor ten, I give you that, yeah. But it's nothing to be scared of. I mean, at the end of the day, it's just a picture.'

And he sounded so convincing that she almost believed him.

'A scarily odd picture, mind you,' he added, not very helpfully.

Against her better judgment, Rose looked back at it. The portrait. Hanging on the wall amidst all these Leonardos and Cezannes and Gauguins and What-Have-Yous. A portrait of herself. Screaming. And screaming, it seemed to Rose, for her very life.

'WHY ARE WE GOING TO AN ART gallery then?' Rose had asked.

'What's the matter? Don't you like art galleries?'

'Not much,' sniffed Rose. 'Went to one on a school trip. The floors squeaked. And everyone whispered. And we weren't allowed to touch anything.'

'Oh, I *love* art galleries,' grinned the Doctor, as he set the TARDIS controls. 'Big long tall echoey rooms, you've got to love the echoes. And the lemon cheesecake in the café is always good. Portions are too small and it's a bit overpriced, but art gallery lemon cheesecakes are the best lemon cheesecakes in the universe.'

Rose smiled and rolled her eyes. 'And then there's the art?'

'Yeah, the art's pretty good too.'

ROSE HAD HOPED THAT ON her first trip to the moon she'd get to bounce about in low gravity and do the whole 'one small step for man' thing. Instead her first impressions of it, as the TARDIS materialised in the foyer of the Mons Herodotus wing, was that it was dark and empty. 'Must be early closing,' she said. 'How big is this place?'

'Oh, the gallery doesn't cover the entire moon. Nah, they've dug out the Sea of Tranquillity and turned it into a gift shop. Oh, listen, Rose,' cried the Doctor. 'I was right. *Hello-o!* Hear that? *Hello-o-o-o!*'

The Doctor showed Rose into the glass capsule by the doorway. 'Right,' he said. 'You push a button here, and it'll speed us to whichever part of the gallery you want to visit. Say, y'know, you fancy seventeenth century Venetian landscapes – and why not, all those canals and ruffs, what's not to like? – you punch it into this terminal here, and we'd be there in a flash. We could be enjoying seventeenth century Venetian landscapes in just about as long as it takes to say 'seventeenth century Venetian landscapes'. So. Where d'you want to go?'

Rose smiled. 'Let's go where you want to go.' And she entered the coordinates.

'How did you guess?'

'And maybe afterwards we could try out some modern art. I mean, really *really* modern. Why, don't you like it?'

The Doctor was wrinkling up his nose. 'S'okay,' he said, 'but they use computers.' And the capsule was in flight. From standing to – what? a hundred miles per hour, two hundred, in less than a second. 'Oh my God,' was all Rose could manage, as the G-force hit her. The Doctor didn't even seem to notice. 'I've got nothing against computers,' he said. 'Some of my best friends are computers. And if a computer fancies a go at some art, then good luck to it. But when they're just used to make art, then I think something gets lost along the way. Don't you think so? I do.'

'.......' said Rose, gulping for air like a goldfish. 'I know what you're going to say, yeah, if the pictures look just as good, what does it matter if they're done with a paintbrush or with a keyboard? And it's a fair point, Rose, good one. But I don't think the ends ever justify the means. Not even on this scale. Do you? Oh, watch out for this bit, there's a fast swerve around...'

'*Aaaaaaarghhh...!*'

'...that bunch of craters. For me, those paintings seem

a bit soulless. You know, no life in them. Now, some artists realised this problem, tried to get around it. Really wanted to put themselves into their art. Began using Soul Extractors, siphoning off bits of their soul, then pumping it into the canvas. Seems a bit silly to me, I mean, come on, if you'll go to those lengths, why not just use a pencil and draw it yourself? Ah,' he said, as the shuttle came to an abrupt halt, and Rose felt her stomach catch up with the rest of her body an uncomfortably long couple of seconds later, 'seventeenth century Venetian.' He beamed. 'We can walk from here.'

But they didn't spend long in that exhibition; even the Doctor admitted he'd got a bit canalled and ruffed out. He seemed worried that the gallery was deserted. 'It shouldn't be closed, though,' he grumbled as they sped their way to Twenty-Second Century Neo-Cubism. 'They've taken all the art and stuck it on the moon, the least they can do is make sure it's easy to get at when you want to. The Earth's gonna be pretty grey without it.'

Rose rather liked the fact they were on their own. She still felt a bit self-conscious talking at normal volume – she half-expected some teacher was going to shush her – but it meant she was free to enjoy the pictures at her own pace. And she'd been wrong – there was plenty to touch. Underneath each frame was a little button, and if she pressed it an electronic voice was all too eager to give her information on who painted the picture in question, what paint he'd used, what he'd been thinking at the time, and no doubt even what his shoe size had been. (But Rose noted, with not a little smugness, she had been right about one thing… the floors did squeak.)

All in all, she was enjoying herself much more than she expected. Pictures were a lot more interesting when there wasn't someone over your shoulder saying you *had* to enjoy them… or else. There was a Rubens she liked, and a Breughel, and a Gibbons, and a Van Gogh.

She'd relaxed enough that when she saw the picture of herself it took a moment to dawn on her that she was actually very frightened indeed.

It was just below the enormous picture of King Carl XVII of the Scandinavian Union, resplendent on his robot horse and grinning oafishly through a thick moustache.

It wasn't very big or very grand. It'd have been easy to have missed it altogether, dwarfed as it was by the portraits of members of the twenty-fourth century's minor royalty.

But it was her. Absolutely her. It was like looking in a mirror. The shape of the face, the cut of the hair. Rose Tyler, absolutely.

Except for one thing. This Rose looked terrified. Her face was contorted in a scream, the mouth twisted unnaturally to let it out.

The artist had caught that moment of terror perfectly, every single nuance of it. And rather than help her, this artist had stood by, no, worse – he'd observed her carefully, studied her, then slapped what he saw on canvas. And with an accuracy that was cruel, *had* to be deliberately cruel… Rose felt she was looking on the moment of her own death – surely that's what it had to be, what else could produce an expression of such horror? And then it was all she could do not to scream too, scream like her portrait, scream the whole art gallery down. Instead, as calmly as she could, she just said, 'Doctor.'

The Doctor had been practising his echo again. But as soon as he heard the controlled steel in Rose's voice, he was by her side.

'I suppose,' said Rose at last, 'that it might not be me at all. I mean, it could just be a coincidence.'

'Well,' said the Doctor, 'yeah… Yeah, it'd be a pretty big coincidence, though. A whopping great coincidence. I think on the Coincidence Scale, a factor of eleven. And, like the Oddness Scale, it only goes up to ten. No, no, I don't think it's a coincidence. Rose… she's wearing the same clothes you're wearing now.'

Rose saw he was right. So intent had she been on the screaming face she hadn't bothered to look at the blue zip-up top underneath. Somehow, it was that that made her shudder.

'You all right?' asked the Doctor. 'It's going to be okay, Rose. Whatever this is, I promise, I'm not going to let anything happen to you.'

'I know you won't,' she said, and managed a smile. 'It's just that… what sort of artist would do that?'

'Let's find out,' said the Doctor. And he stabbed at the information button.

The computer voice chirped up. '*Title: Untitled.*'

'Not very imaginative,' muttered the Doctor.

'*Would you like some more information?*'

'Yes. Who painted it would be good for starters.'

'*Artist: Unknown. Would you like some more information?*'

'Give me everything you've got.'

'*Date of composition: Unknown. School or Genre: Unknown. Influences: Unknown. Anecdotal Information: Unknown.*'

'All right,' snapped the Doctor. 'That's enough.'

Rose gave a nervous smile. 'Looks like he doesn't want to own up to it.'

'Nah, there's something wrong with this information terminal. A gallery like this will have the whole catalogue on record. We'll just have to find one. Come on,' he said, taking her hand, 'we'll pop down to the gift shop, solve this little mystery. It's only a picture,' he added seriously. 'I know it's frightening, but it's just a picture. A bit of paint on a bit of canvas. It can't hurt you.'

Rose nodded, the Doctor smiled, and they walked back to the shuttle. He wanted to get Rose as far away from the picture as possible. Before she looked into the eyes of that portrait a little too long,

and saw something he didn't want to have to explain. That in that portrait of Rose… screaming with such fury… the eyes were quite, quite mad. Whatever had frightened Rose so badly, it had also driven her insane.

'Just a picture,' he repeated. 'It can't hurt anyone.'

※ ♔ ※

MIND YOU, THAT WAS BEFORE THEY FOUND ALL the bodies.

'Oh,' said the Doctor. 'This is worse than I thought.'

'What happened to them?' asked Rose, staring.

At first she wasn't even sure they really were bodies. They might have just been statues. Brightly coloured statues, the faces and clothes red and green and pink and blue, as if they'd been designed by a baby with a crayon and an attitude. Statues of people browsing postcards in the gift shop, statues of shop assistants behind the cash registers. Their too ripe, too shiny sheen looked thick and artificial, even in the half light.

'It's like someone's thrown a bucket of paint over them,' said Rose. But it wasn't, really. It was like someone had thrown a thousand buckets of paint over them. Enough paint to make sure that it had covered every square inch of their bodies. Rose felt certain that it wasn't just on the outside either – these people were full of paint, as if they'd drunk it until they could literally hold no more, as if every spare nook or cranny inside that might have been used for bones or blood had been replaced by this thick stickiness.

And on every face was a scream. And, Rose saw with shock, it was the same scream. All of them exactly the same expression – the eyes bulging to just the same degree, the throats equally taut and strained. The scream on her own portrait, in fact – copied and duplicated onto all these poor people. 'What killed them?' she heard herself ask numbly.

Grimly the Doctor studied the face of a woman who had been browsing the fridge magnets. 'There's still a pulse in there.'

'They're alive?'

'If you can call it that.'

Behind the counter stood a girl. A giddy fusion of dusky orange and aquamarine, with random splodges of green. She could hardly have been older than Rose. Perhaps it was her first job after she'd left school – perhaps, as Rose had promised herself when she took the job at Henrik's, it was a stop-gap until she found something better. She wouldn't find anything better now; whatever it was she had dreamed of, it had been cut short by something impossible and weird and stupid. 'I'm sorry,' Rose said helplessly. She didn't know if she could feel the cold, or a need for comfort, or anything, come to that. But she put her hand on the girl's shoulder anyway.

'Don't!' yelled the Doctor, but it was too late. The girl's shoulders shivered, and the shiver turned into a wobble, and for a moment the whole body was wobbling like a multicoloured jelly. And then her entire body collapsed, as if the whole thing had been made of nothing more solid than water – as if it had been impossible it could have stayed upright in the first place, and it took Rose's touch to remind it of that.

The girl splashed on to the floor into a shiny puddle.

Rose cried out.

'No, watch,' said the Doctor.

The puddle was running back together again, all the liquid racing back over the floor, and reforming itself into the shape of a body. As if it were filling up an invisible mould, the paint became legs once more, then a torso, then a chest…

'Whatever's doing this, it's trying to preserve these people as best it can,' said the Doctor. 'But why? What's going on?'

'Doctor,' said Rose. 'The face.'

The shop assistant's body was complete. But with one difference. The paint had grown back into that taut neck, the twisted mouth, the bulging eyes. But it was Rose's face. Rose's scream.

'I've had a nasty thought,' said the Doctor.

'Yeah, I'm having a fair few of them myself.'

'Maybe the art gallery wasn't closed to stop people getting in. Maybe… it was to stop the art getting out.' He strode over to the catalogue, flicked through its pages. 'I really must stop having nasty thoughts, cos they almost always turn out to be right.' He looked at the book, then tossed it away. 'Let's get back to your portrait.'

'Does it say what it's called?'

'Untitled.'

'Just like before.'

'Not quite,' said the Doctor. 'Every single picture in the catalogue is now untitled too. Since we've arrived it's erased the identity of everything in here.' He broke into a run. 'I don't think we've got much time left.'

'YOU'RE GONNA WISH I HADN'T SAID THIS,' muttered the Doctor. 'But you know the way that eyes in pictures seem to follow you about the room?' He looked around him, down the long hall, at the hundreds of portraits it held. 'Well, I think they really are.'

'You're right. I wish you hadn't said that.'

'Sorry.'

The eye thing was a bit off-putting, Rose had to admit. The way the faces seemed more alive than before, the way they stared down at the Doctor, wanting something – wanting what? But that was nothing to the fact that now every single face on those pictures was hers. An art gallery full of Rose Tylers. It would almost have been flattering – except for the fact that none of those faces seemed altogether happy at the transformation, screaming away like that. King Carl XVII still boasted his manly moustache, but now the features behind the bristles were altogether more feminine. And the robo-horse he sat on now just looked like Rose Tyler with a muzzle.

Rose would have laughed out loud at them both had she not been so terrified.

'I think it's trying to communicate,' said the Doctor. 'Reaching out to us. Just like it reached out to those people in the gift shop. That's why it took your face. Why it's made everything else here take it too. If this gallery's been quarantined as long as I think, you might have been the first new creature it'd seen in quite a while.'

'Okay,' said Rose. 'Then why's it screaming?'

'I don't know,' said the Doctor. 'Whatever it wants, it must want it very badly. What could an untitled little picture like you be after, eh?' He looked at the portrait hard for a few moments,

as if willing it to call it quits and just tell him. 'Maybe it's not screaming at all,' he said at last.

'Look at it! What else could it be?'

'Well, from our perspective, that picture looks static, doesn't it? Not moving at all. But we know there's something alive in there. Maybe it is moving. Just very… very… slowly.' He stared at the picture again. 'That mouth. It's not in the same position it was in when we first came here.'

Rose looked at the scream, fighting down the sick giddiness she felt whenever she looked at it too closely. 'Seems the same to me.'

'The lips are a bit closer together, look. The tongue has risen slightly. One of your incisors has been covered up, just a smidgen, see?'

'Pity, one of my best features…'

He beamed at her, excited. 'It's not screaming,' he said. 'That mouth is shaping words. Just at a speed we can't decipher.'

Rose wondered what a picture of herself in an art gallery on the moon could possibly be wanting to chat about, but didn't dare say it aloud in case it came out all hysterical and embarrassing.

'Thing is, being a Time Lord… I'm supposed to be able to be good at things like this. Give time a bit of a nudge.' He flexed his hands.

'Isn't that dangerous?'

'Yeah.' And before he changed his mind, he wrenched the picture off the wall, grasping its frame as tightly as he could.

Its eyes rolled and looked at him.

He gave a cry, fell to his knees.

'Doctor!' Rose rushed to his side.

'It's very strong,' he said between gritted teeth. 'I knew it would be, but not like this… No, don't touch me. Just watch it,

watch its lips,
watch what it says...!

The face was shouting,
desperate and scared. The wide-opened
mouth she'd taken for a scream closing, the lips
then puckering, another syllable being formed. Then opening
again in a different position altogether, as if the face were trying
to whistle. No sound, just the shape of conversation. Three
syllables, over and over again, Rose's face shouting at her
silently. For a few moments, as the Doctor grabbed on to the
frame with all his might, Rose thought she wouldn't be able to
work out what it was saying. But then it clicked in her head –
am I who am I who am I who am I who...

The Doctor could hold on no longer. The portrait fell to the
ground. The glass smashed.

'Look,' shouted Rose.

Paint was running down the walls. Long streams of it, like
multicoloured tendrils, leaking out of each picture and
gathering in large pools on
the floor. It was as if every single portrait was bleeding in
sympathy. King Carl looked sad and grotesque as his borrowed
face caved in and elongated, stretched like a piece of chewing
gum, before it dribbled out of the picture altogether; the robo-
horse was long gone and part of the puddle that was now
flowing its way towards the Doctor and Rose.

They turned around, but there was nowhere to run. From all
sides the sticky dregs of the art gallery was slurping in their
direction. 'It knew I was trying to reach out to it. Now it's
returning the favour.' The slow tidal wave rolled ever closer.

'Whoops.'

'What does it want?'

'This must have been what happened before. To all those people downstairs. The paint wanted to chat, and didn't realise its own strength. It absorbed them. Don't let it touch you. You saw what happened if you let it touch you.'

Rose couldn't see she'd have much choice – another few moments and it'd be lapping at her feet. 'What are we gonna do?'

The Doctor hesitated for a second. Then, 'Let it touch me,' he said, and dived straight in.

THE DOCTOR HAD LONG AGO DECIDED IT WASN'T worth worrying too much when he got imprisoned. He'd been imprisoned for so long and so often that it almost always felt like business as usual, whatever the size of the cell, and whether it be in deep space or at the back of the shopping centre in Putney. He'd even been imprisoned inside a drawing before, and he'd escaped to tell the tale. But this... this was rather odder.

And if the Doctor thought about it too directly, he realised he was actually frightened.

It was a strange feeling to be part of a painting. There he'd been all these years, merrily

travelling through time and relative dimensions. And here he was now, two dimensions only, flat as a pancake, paint to the left of him, paint to the right, paint right through him come to think of it.

He hoped he'd be able to get out again.

He felt the voice throughout his whole body. No, it wasn't exactly a voice – more like an itch, as if every bit of his skin had suddenly developed the same urgent itch. 'Who am I?'

'I don't know,' he replied, honestly.

'Who am I?'

'No-one knows who you are. You're untitled.'

'Who am I? Who am I? Who am I?'

The Doctor looked about him. For a moment he thought he was standing in a summer's field. Then he was in a bowl of flowers. Then a hair on the head of the Mona Lisa. He supposed that the creature had tried out every single picture within the gallery in search for some identity. It was all these pictures at once – and yet none of them at all.

The Doctor could see how it happened now. He'd had his suspicions, but now he was the picture, the picture was him, and he could see more clearly. Some artist who tried just too hard, who wanted to put a bit too much of himself into his work. Got a bit carried away with the Soul Extractor. He probably just wanted to paint the best picture he could, but instead he'd created something that was alive. And alive without ever knowing what it was. Stuck behind glass, fixed on a wall, gawped at by millions of strangers, and left forever to ponder what on earth it might be.

'Who am I?'

But none of this gave the Doctor an answer to that buzzing insistent question crawling all over his skin. Who am I, who am I?

Pretty soon it was the only thing the Doctor could think. He realised with a moment's horror that everything else was being wiped away, that there was nothing else. Come to think of it, who was he? He hadn't a clue.

He knew there was something important he was meant to be doing. And he idly wondered what it could be. It was important, cos he owed it to... someone else... outside the picture. And that was ludicrous, cos there was no outside, the picture was everything! But with every last effort of his will... he turned his head. Not to the left. Not to the right. But somewhere impossible inbetween.

He stared out of the canvas. Life out there whirled by far too quickly – sped-up to a blur. But he was a Time Lord, wasn't he? (*who am I?*), he was supposed to be able to make sense of all that chaos. If only he could be sure (*who am I?*) what a Time Lord actually was, was he even sure (*who*) that he'd heard the expression before (*am*), that it even had anything to do with him in the first place (*I who am*), whoever he was, who was he, he wondered, who am I?

But the more he concentrated the more the blur seemed to steady, and he could make out a shape through all the rush. There was a girl looking in at him, so scared – yeah, scared but so brave, and there was a name to go with that girl, Rose Tyler. He didn't know his own name any more (*WHO AM I?*) but he knew her, she was Rose Tyler and she was the most important thing to him. She was Rose and he was the Doctor, yeah, Rose and the Doctor. Rose was his best friend and his job was to protect her. Rose and the Doctor (*who am I?*), the Doctor and Rose, it went together like bangers and mash, fish and chips (*who am I? I'm the Doctor!*). Rose defined him, and he was the Doctor, he was the Doctor, and he wouldn't forget again.

He gasped for breath. 'I know who I am.'

And at last the questions stopped.

'I'm the Doctor,' he said. 'And I'm going to help you.'

And the voice. Gentle this time. Like a small child. 'And who am I?'

The Doctor took a deep breath. 'Well, if you want my opinion... I think you're old enough to decide that for yourself.'

⊛ ⊛ ⊛

'LEMON CHEESECAKE?' SAID ROSE.

'Yeah.'

'It's a picture of a lemon cheesecake.'

The Doctor and Rose were looking at the little picture, back in its rightful place, nestled beneath the feet of King Carl. Both Carl and his mechanical steed were as masculine and as equine as they were meant to be. Once the Doctor had helped the picture work out a new identity for itself, all the paint had simply flowed back into position again.

'It didn't know what it was,' the Doctor explained, 'and once it touched anything, it couldn't be sure that wasn't part of it too. It'll keep itself to itself from now on, now that it's worked out where its body ends and everybody else's begins.'

'So the people downstairs...?'

'Will be fine. And if they're lucky, they might even be the right colour.'

Rose looked at the picture. She had to admit it was an especially nice looking cheesecake. 'If it was its own decision... how come it's changed into something *you* like?'

The Doctor blustered a bit. 'We had a long chat about it. And I admit I did point out that cheesecake was a particularly good thing to aspire to. But the picture realised that, of all the different shapes it had ever tried wearing, it had never been one of those. Just think, Rose, art gallery the size of a moon. And never an example of cheesecake art.' He grinned. ''Til now, that is.'

'And what if it gets fed up being a lemon cheesecake?'

'I suppose it'll change its flavour.' Rose looked unconvinced, so the Doctor said seriously, 'Look, it's happy now. It never wanted to take over the universe, it just wanted to find out what it was, and what it was for. That's better than most lifeforms get. If I hadn't found out what I was for, I'd never have made it out of there.'

'So,' said Rose, 'what did you find out? What *are* you for?' But the Doctor just smiled and took her hand. And before he led her back to the TARDIS, he pushed the information button.

The little computer voice chattered happily:

'*School or genre: Bakery confectionery.*

'*Artist: Itself, thank you very much.*

'*Title: Factor Eleven on the Oddness Scale.*'

THE
END

No One Died

WRITTEN BY **NICHOLAS BRIGGS**   ILLUSTRATIONS BY **BEN WILLSHER**

'WANT ONE?'

Rose turned to the Doctor with a bit of a start. The door of the tiny shop rattled shut behind him. He was proffering two small ice lollies.

'What are they?' she asked.

'Sky Rays. Sky Rays are good. What were you looking at?'

'I dunno... Just... the people, I s'pose.'

'They look happy enough, don't they?' he said, having finished blowing into the lolly's paper wrapper, inflating it away from the ice.

'And you're sure no one died?'

The Doctor nodded, his tongue now slightly stuck to the lolly. Rose couldn't restrain a smirk.

'I'm a bit out of practice with Sky Rays,' he smiled, his tongue already stained a deep orange.

Rose unwrapped her lolly, tasted it, thought it was disgusting, but pretended she liked it, just for the Doctor's sake. He knew she was fibbing and encouraged her to chuck the lolly into a street-side bin on the way back to the TARDIS.

⊕ ⊕ ⊕

THE DOCTOR HAD EXPLAINED that in 1962, the English village of Lower Downham had vanished. One day, it wasn't on the maps any more. And soon after, the only people who still remembered it were conspiracy theorists who mainly lived in sheds.

There had been no missing persons reports filed, no police investigations and the Doctor had never had a clue as to what had actually happened. It seemed that not a living soul had so much as raised an eyebrow at the mysterious erasure of Lower Downham.

'So, first stop –'

'Lower Downham,' grinned Rose, leaning on the TARDIS' control console, awaiting the Doctor's customary flurry of activity at the point of dematerialisation.

'Before, during and after,' confirmed the Doctor. 'But not necessarily in that order!'

So, the TARDIS had arrived in Lower Downham before the little village had disappeared. It was a quaint, unremarkable place. Sky Rays were on sale. The postman had a limp. The police constable was a bit too fat to ride his bike without wobbling. The local children wore short trousers, woolly jumpers and played conkers. Rose had rather liked the look of the clock tower. There seemed to be something oddly reassuring about its faded, green-ish copper dome.

On the way back to the TARDIS, after the disposal of Rose's Sky Ray, the Doctor had bought a local Ordinance Survey map.

And there was Lower Downham, as plain as could be, tucked behind Downham Wood, bordering the Ainsworth Bypass.

⊗ ☻ ⊗

WHEN THE TARDIS NEXT MATERIALISED, THE DOCTOR was aiming for a bold entrance. He would try to get his ship to land right in the middle of the High Street.

'And this is... *after* the village disappeared, right?' asked Rose, just starting to worry that the Doctor was going to get them lost in some sort of home counties Bermuda Triangle.

'That's the theory,' said the Doctor, grinning with mischievous intensity.

'And... no one died?' Rose asked again.

'No one died. Just a harmless little mystery.' The Doctor said happily, his fingers dancing over the controls.

'Okay, just checking.' Rose didn't mind a harmless little mystery. Harmless was good. It just never seemed to happen around the Doctor...

The TARDIS landed with a resounding thud.

'I'm getting a hint of 'not totally convinced' from you,' commented the Doctor.

'Me? No!'

'All right...' said the Doctor, not totally convinced.

By the time they exited the TARDIS, he was thoroughly disgruntled. They had not landed in the High Street, they were in Downham Wood. Rose pulled the map from her jeans' pocket. The sun was low in the sky, so they both squinted as they tried to work out their position.

Somehow, the map had folded right in the middle of the village. It was as though the print had spilled into a dark dip in the paper. The Doctor attempted to illuminate it with the neon glow of his sonic screwdriver, but its light seemed too bright for the faded print, making it, if anything, even more difficult to read.

They walked around for a while, through the quiet wood, but never seemed to be able to choose the right direction.

'This is weird,' said Rose, stopping in frustration. 'It's like... we keep taking a wrong turning.'

'Yeah we do, don't we...?' the Doctor pondered.

Rose had already made a decision. She was heading for the TARDIS. The Doctor raced to catch up with her.

Determined, tramping through the undergrowth, she said, 'I've had it with the "before" and the "after".' This harmless little mystery was evidently starting to get to her. The Doctor gave a secret smile.

'Time for the "during"?' he suggested, with all the innocence he could muster. He didn't really need to ask.

🕐 🕑 🕒

THIS TIME, THE TARDIS LANDED RIGHT UNDER THE clock tower.

'Did you aim for night time?' asked Rose, feeling a little unnerved by the lack of limping postmen, fat bobbys and conkers.

'TARDIS clock says it's three o'clock in the afternoon,' said the Doctor.

'So does that.' Rose was looking up at the clock tower. 'Unless it's three in the morning?' The tower was looking unnervingly gothic and unfriendly now. There was a moonlit sky behind it, but no sign of the moon.

'Anyone at home?' the Doctor suddenly called out. Rose instinctively clutched his arm.

'Is that a good idea?' she whispered.

'Well... remember, no one died,' he said, breezily, striding off towards the Sky Ray shop.

'As long as that includes us...' she muttered to herself, gingerly following him, her eyes darting about the High Street. The buzz of the sonic screwdriver signalled that the Doctor was forcing the lock of the shop.

With a gentle tinkling of the shop's bell, the Doctor had vanished inside. But as Rose moved to join him, she caught a flashing movement out of the corner of her eye. She instinctively stopped and turned. Nothing there.

Then a sound. A faint, distant fizz of a sound. Electrical? Maybe... The word 'Doctor' was just forming in her mouth as the sound came again, and this time the flashing was up close and blinding.

Winded and knocked a little senseless, Rose was suddenly carried away on something bright, fizzing and immensely fast. Within a second, she was gone from the High Street.

'Freezer's off. Sky Rays are melting,' said the Doctor as he exited the shop. Then he saw that Rose had gone.

He looked up and down the street. Called her name. He ran back to the TARDIS, went inside, checked she wasn't there. Out again, into the street. No Rose.

'No one died,' he reassured himself, and then he saw something. A glowing figure, right at the other end of the street. It was like it had been caught in a solitary beam from the non-existent moon. Glowing white, vaguely human-shaped, it seemed to be facing away from the Doctor.

But then it turned... And started to walk towards him. A slow, determined pace. The Doctor tensed himself for a confrontation, but stayed close to the TARDIS door.

As the figure approached, the differences between it and a human being became more apparent. About eight feet tall, it had hunched, rounded shoulders which appeared to connect with the back of the head. No neck. And the head itself was an outsized oval which seemed to be made of two imperfectly connected halves. There was a definite joining line in the middle which ran right down to the point where the front of the head buried itself into the creature's partially inflated-looking chest. And no facial features, except for a rectangular slit, somewhere near where human eyes might have been.

Inside that slit, darkness.

The creature raised what looked like an old fashioned Geiger counter. A box with some kind of probe attached by a wire. It held the box in one mitten-like hand and presented the probe with the other, pointing it directly at the Doctor.

In response, he raised his sonic screwdriver, but found himself unable to resist as the figure stopped in front of him and gently brushed his screwdriver arm aside. The probe moved ever closer to the Doctor's eyes, and everything went dark.

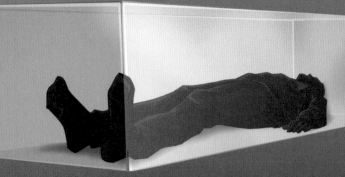

ROSE FOUND HERSELF FALLING TO THE GROUND, her dazzling journey at breakneck speed was over. Fighting to regain her senses, she felt soft grass beneath her. She was on the village green. She'd seen the local bobby cycle uncertainly past the local war memorial, near here, on her first trip to the village. She looked around, trying to get her bearings. Where was the memorial?

But all she could see was a mass of what looked like gleaming glass, sparkling in the unreal moonlight. The memorial must be behind that, she thought. And then she caught sight of what had brought her here. A cuboid, glass object... about the size of a coffin. And as if to underline the fact, she could see a human body, prone inside it.

Scrambling to her feet, she watched as the object hovered about ten feet off the ground and gently inserted itself into a gap in the glass mass. Suddenly, another glass cuboid rocketed past and came to an abrupt halt in mid air, also inserting itself into the structure. It dawned on Rose that she had been accidentally propelled here by a flying coffin whose mission was apparently to join up with...

And then she was close enough to see.

The entire glass mass was made up of hundreds of these coffins, all of them with the dark blur of a body inside. She ran forward. It was like a vast, hovering, fizzing glass sculpture. Peering inside the nearest few coffins, she could see a young boy in a woolly jumper and shorts, a conker lying beside him. Above him, the lady who'd sold them the map. Further back, the unmistakable bulk of a large policeman, still wearing his helmet.

At that moment, she spotted a white, distorted reflection in the glass. Rose turned and saw three, tall, white figures advancing towards her. No faces, bulbous oval heads, hunched shoulders and arms outstretched holding things that looked like they could be weapons, or microphones or...

But as they reached her, Rose felt all her will to question, to run or to fight just ebb away.

Fighting against the overwhelming tide of indifference smothering her thoughts, she managed to blurt out, 'No one was supposed to die! But you've killed them! You've–'

THE DOCTOR'S EYES BLINKED OPEN JUST IN TIME TO see something that looked like a hovering glass coffin lowering itself onto him. In a moment, he had rolled away and clambered to his feet.

The white figure standing nearby, seemingly supervising the operation, jerked its head round in what looked like surprise.

'Yeah, I know it worked for a while,' said the Doctor, idly tapping the coffin, then pressing it to ascertain the force of its hovering power, 'but my brain's wired a bit differently. I'm not from round here. Is that a gun? I don't think it's a gun. Tell me it's not a gun.'

The creature was pointing the probe at him again.

'No, whatever it is, it won't work again, so why don't you just make this simple and answer all my questions? What d'you say?' The Doctor smiled his best smile.

The creature lowered its probe.

'I'll take that as a yes. So, why did you make this village disappear? Why is it night time in the middle of the afternoon and, most importantly to me just now,' the smile fell from his face, 'where's Rose Tyler?'

He raised his sonic screwdriver. The creature instantly flinched and stepped back. Innocently, the Doctor redirected his device at the hovering coffin.

'Some kind of stasis device?' he asked, noting a few inconclusive readings. 'Can't see how it hovers. Must be something very clever. That means you must be something very clever, so come on, answer the questions before one of us gets a bit cross. Actually, that'll be me. I'll be getting a bit cross.'

The creature slowly put its Geiger counter apparatus down. When it was standing upright again, it stretched out a hand to the Doctor. He eyed it suspiciously.

'Now what?'

As if in answer, the mittened hand started to undulate in a subtle, complex fashion. The Doctor beamed.

'Blimey, it's ages since I've seen that!' he gasped, excitedly. 'Go on, do it again!'

No response.

'Oh, hold on!' The Doctor pocketed his sonic screwdriver, then, after a moment's thought, stretched out his arm and started making subtle, undulating movements with his right hand.

'Any good? Am I making sense?' he asked, hopefully. 'Or have I just insulted your mother?'

As if magnetic poles had suddenly been reversed and attraction changed to repulsion, the glass structure separated with a speed and force that literally knocked the attendant Viyrans flat on their backs. As soon as they recovered, they started running uncertainly in all directions.

Rose and the Doctor couldn't resist a grin. It all looked rather comic. But then the smiles were wiped from their faces by their immediate problems. They were shooting along at what felt to Rose like about a hundred miles per hour. Somehow, the Doctor was holding their caskets together with his sonic screwdriver.

Despite their predicament, she managed to roll her eyes at the sight of his cheeky grin and cocky wink as he braced himself against the velocity, steadfastly holding the screwdriver. Alarmingly, the alignment of the caskets started to slip and Rose smashed her hand through to grab the Doctor.

'Oops, now you've done it!' he cried out as the glass disintegrated around them and they fell to Earth.

Dazed and bruised, they staggered to their feet and nearly got hit by several more caskets whizzing past. A Viyran thundered past in pursuit, momentarily noticing them, but clearly feeling the pursuit of the caskets was more important.

'It's mayhem!' laughed Rose as she ducked to dodge another one. 'Will they get it under control?'

'Well, they *are* very clever,' said the Doctor, pointing up the road ahead of them. There was the clock tower, suddenly looking very inviting, and beneath it, the reassuring blue shape of the TARDIS. Instinctively, they grabbed one another's hands and ran for home.

But just as they were about to reach safety, TARDIS key in the Doctor's hand, a casket swept in front of them, barring their way. A Viyran strode forward, apparently holding the casket in place with its probe-like device.

'Oh dear,' said the Doctor, surprisingly sympathetically, Rose thought. 'That's not going to work. I said...' And he started hand-signing.

'What are you saying?' whispered Rose.

'I said, "That's not going to work".' And there was that smile again.

'I know you said that, but what did you say to him?'

'That's not going to work.'

'Oh,' said Rose. 'Isn't it?'

'Never in a month of Sundays,' he confirmed. 'Hmm, don't know how to sign that.'

And then the casket shot off down the road. The Viyran's head jerked towards the Doctor. The probe menacingly outstretched towards them...

'Look, I know you're cross, but...' the Doctor signed something quickly and the Viyran stopped in his tracks. It looked down the street at the escaping casket and pointed its probe.

In that split second, the Doctor pulled Rose into the TARDIS.

WITHOUT A MOMENT'S HESITATION, THE DOCTOR slammed the door and set the TARDIS in motion. Rose found the shudder of power and the creaking of the old time ship's bones infinitely comforting.

'You wanna know what I said to him, don't you?' asked the Doctor, his face aglow with light from the console.

'In your own time,' said Rose, smirking. 'Actually, I don't care.'

'Don't you now?' teased the Doctor. 'What *do* you care about, then?'

'No one died,' she said. 'Though I was a bit worried we might be the exceptions.'

'Yeah, well, technically we could have been,' he admitted.

'What, you mean we were in danger? Now there's a surprise,' Rose laughed, sinking into the Doctor's chair.

'Oh, and I gave that Viyran the correct atomic weights for him to reconfigure the caskets into that structure again,' the Doctor said, as if he was just making idle conversation, continuing with his flurry of control adjustments.

'Aren't you the clever one,' she said. 'But answer me this – why was it dark at three o'clock in the afternoon?'

The Doctor stopped dead. And in that instant, Rose knew she'd flummoxed him.

'Aha!' she grinned. 'Gotcha!'

'Well, we could always go back and find out,' he suggested, moving his hand as if to reverse the co-ordinates.

Rose leapt forward and slapped his hand flat on the console.

'Don't you dare!' she said, and didn't let go of his hand for quite a while.

Corner of the Eye

WRITTEN BY **STEVEN MOFFAT** ILLUSTRATIONS BY **DARYL JOYCE**

Warning: Never give out your password or credit card number in an instant message conversation. To help prevent infection by a computer virus or worm, never accept or open any file or link in an instant message until you verify its authenticity with the sender.

KATHY says:
Hiya handsome, how's it going? Haven't seen you on here for AGES! I was starting to worry.

TOM says:
Oh, Kathy, my dear. You've forgotten again, haven't you? Sometimes I can't bear it, I really can't

KATHY says:
Tom? Tom, dear, what are you talking about? Have I done something wrong again? Ooh, Mr. Strict!

TOM says:
You don't remember a thing, do you? None of it. Forgotten it all,

haven't you? Every time, the same!

KATHY says:
Forgotten what? Tom, I honestly don't know what you're on about. Are you having a laugh?

TOM says:
The last time we spoke on here... the last thirty, forty, God knows how many times... remember what I explained to you? Please try.

KATHY says:
I don't remember you explaining anything. Tom, we haven't talked for AGES. Come on, silly sausage, are you having a joke with me?

KATHY says:
Tom, are you there?

KATHY says:
Tom, please, are you there?

KATHY says:

Tom, don't ignore me, I KNOW you're there.

TOM says:

Okay. Let's do it all again. But this time really try. Really try and remember what I'm telling you. Okay? Think you can do that?

KATHY says:

You're scaring me, Tom.

TOM says:

Do you think you can do that?

KATHY says:

Fine, whatever you want. Just stop scaring me!

TOM says:

I need you to concentrate.

KATHY says:

I'll concentrate. Yes sir!! Mad, you are.

TOM says:

I'm going to ask you a question. Want you to think very carefully about the answer, okay?

KATHY says:

Okay.

TOM says:

You're going to be a little bit scared when you think about this question. I need you to stay calm, and stay with me. Okay?

KATHY says:

Ooh, Mr Mysterious!

TOM says:

Where are you?

KATHY says:

Where am I? Is that it?

TOM says:

Yes. Where are you? Describe to me the room you're sitting in.

KATHY says:

The room has three yellow walls and one blue wall. The room is 12 feet by 8 feet. The room has one door. The room has no windows. The room has four lights. The room has seven chairs. The room has two light switches.

TOM says:

Read back what you've written. That's not a description. It's a list of facts. I want you to DESCRIBE the room. What it looks, what it FEELS like, what you can see, smell, touch. Can you do that?

TOM says:

Kathy, are you there? Can you do that, describe the room? Don't be afraid.

KATHY says:

Oh my God.

TOM says:

Stay with me, stay calm.

KATHY says:

Oh my God, Tom! I can't see ANYTHING. Not even blackness. Nothing. I can't feel, I can't touch. Tom, where am I? I don't understand, it's like I'm not anywhere. I can't see, I can't feel, I can't

touch. I don't even know how I'm typing this. Please, Tom, WHERE AM I???

TOM says:

Calm, remember. Calm as you can be. Focus on my words. I'm going to tell you a story. It's not the first time I've told it to you. Won't be the last, I shouldn't think. It's going to scare you, at times – it always scares you – but I'm here and I'm not going anywhere. I promise.

KATHY says:

Where am I, Tom?? What's happened to me, WHERE AM I???

TOM says:

Hush. Calm. Got to be calm, Kathy.

KATHY says::
Please. I don't understand where I am. Don't go!! Don't log off!

TOM says:
I'm not going anywhere. Now hush. And think back. Do you remember, back when we were together, all that time ago... do you remember the bathroom mirror?

KATHY says:
Never mind your stupid mirror, what's happened to me??

TOM says:
Please, just do as I ask. Do you remember the mirror? It's important.

KATHY says:
The big thing. With that horrid gold frame. In that creepy bathroom at the top of the house. I hated that bathroom.

TOM says:
That's it, the big mirror with the gold frame. And the crack, remember the crack? You always wanted me to get it fixed. I said I was used to the crack and I'd shave all wrong. Okay, that mirror – that big gold mirror, with the crack across the corner – that's where it all begins. Me shaving in the mirror. I want you to imagine me shaving. Picture it. It'll help you to keep hold if you picture things.

KATHY says:
Hold of what?

TOM says:
Picture me standing there, just shaving as normal. It's a beautiful day outside. Sunlight streaming in, birds twittering, God in his heaven, me in my pyjamas. I was probably whistling. And then – it's such a small thing, it makes me want to laugh – I dropped my shaving brush. You wouldn't think your whole world could change because you drop a shaving brush, but thinking back, that was the very last moment of my ordinary life. Clunk on the floor, and a second later everything was different. Because as I bent down to pick up the brush, I saw something in the mirror.

No, not something, let's be exact. I saw a man. A small, neat, perfectly bald man standing directly behind me, and now revealed in the mirror as I bent. I mean right slap behind me, Kathy – his face must've been inches from my shoulder blades, I should've been able to feel his breath on my back.

KATHY says:
My God, Tom!! Who was he, how did he get in??

TOM says:
Coming to that. We locked eyes for just a tiny second. He looked startled, frightened and I imagine I did too. And there we were, in that endless second, staring.

When I say he was small, I don't just mean short – I mean kind of miniature. Like a compacted person, two thirds size; neat, pale, and somehow – the word I want to use is gleaming. Like he was so clean he sparkled. The kind of person – does this make sense? – you look at and know they've got weirdly small hands. I'm always slightly disconcerted by people with very small hands. And he was really THERE, Kathy. I didn't imagine it, it wasn't an illusion – for one totally real moment, he was actually, physically THERE.

This next bit is hard to describe, hard even to remember, because he just sort of – I don't know – *stepped away*. Just slipped out of sight behind me again, but it was so fast and fluid he seemed just to fold out of existence.

And I stood there, shaving foam dripping from my chin, the skin crawling on the back of my neck, and my breath roaring in my ears.

You know, when that kind of thing of happens, for a moment you try and convince yourself you imagined it? Trick of the light, I was telling myself. A waking dream. And then I realized something – something that turned my stomach over. My breath was roaring in my ears, like I told you – but, I suddenly realized, I'd been holding my breath since I saw the man in the mirror. I hadn't dared breathe, since that first moment – so who was breathing now, so close in my ear...

I spun, fast as I could. No one. I spun the other way. No one. But each time, a flicker in the corner of my eye, like a movement so fast it could never be seen. I turned again, again. Each time, nothing. Each time, the flicker. It was odd, that flicker, because it didn't seem like something new. Remember our honeymoon, the fourth night in that hotel, when you said the sound of the waterfall was keeping you awake?

KATHY says:
You said the waterfall had always been there.

TOM says:
And you said, yes, but I've NOTICED it now. It was like that with the flicker. Like it had always been there, but now I'd started noticing it – just the tiniest flicker of someone always stepping out of the way a fraction of a second before I could turn to look. You ever felt that? I think we've all felt that. But for me, it was suddenly, horribly true.

The breathing was returning to normal, softening till I could hardly hear it – like whatever it was that stood just outside my vision was calming itself, returning to normal.

I was frozen again. So afraid, Kathy, I can't describe it.

Finally I spoke – but all I could think to say was "I saw you."

Such a long silence. And then, a soft, girlish, almost falsetto voice, and so horribly close the words were moist on my neck: "It won't happen again."

Kathy, it was like the whole world was reeling around me. Felt like the floor was heaving at my feet, like a sea, about to suck me under. And all I could think was this, these exact words: "I am cursed," I thought. "I've seen what lives in the corner of my eye."

KATHY says:
Oh God, Tom. Tell me it was a dream, tell me you woke up.

TOM says:
I haven't told you the worst yet. I recognized the face. Took me a moment, but standing there, I realized I'd seen that face before, many, many times.

KATHY says:
Where? Tom, where? Tom? Are you still there? Please, I'm alone here, I'm lost in the dark, PLEASE talk to me.

TOM says:
Yes, still here. All these words, takes it out of me. And remembering all this, sometimes it makes me... never mind. You remember the big box of photographs in the hall cupboard?

KATHY says:
I filed and indexed the lot, course I remember.

TOM says:
Course you do. I sat in the middle of the hall floor, and went through every photograph. So many of them, from so long ago. When this big draughty house was full of friends and family and you. There were moments I almost cried.

KATHY says:
But did you find him? Was the little bald man in any of the photographs?

TOM says:
Yes, I found him. I thought I'd been afraid up until that point, but that fear was nothing compared to what I felt now. Yes, Kathy, the little bald man was in the photographs. He was in ALL of them. That is to say, every photograph I had ever taken, or had ever been taken of me, if you looked long enough, and hard enough, you could find him. Sometimes peering out from behind someone with a sly little smile, sometimes reflected in a window, sometimes just a sliver of his bald head peeking over someone's shoulder – every time, somewhere in the photograph, there he was, smiling slyly from every chapter of my life. A numbing certainty grew inside me. The creature, standing inches behind me even as I sorted through the photographs, had been hovering at my shoulder and dancing from my sight all my life.

KATHY says:
Tom, this is impossible. You MUST see that. This is a dream, or some story you've made up. None of this can be true, it's just some horrible fantasy.

TOM says:
And where are you now, Kathy? Is that just some horrible fantasy too? You've got to trust me, or you're never going to understand what's happened to you.

KATHY says:

But it's just so IMPOSSIBLE.

TOM says:

I haven't even mentioned the Doctor yet.

KATHY says:

The Doctor?

TOM says:

Hush. All in good time. The funny thing was, the more I looked at the photos, the less afraid I became. Maybe because it was proof that I hadn't imagined the little man. Perhaps I was, in the end, more afraid of being mad than haunted. I took the best of the photographs down to the kitchen – on the stairs I listened for scurrying behind me, but could hear nothing – and sat at the kitchen table and stared at the little man's face. Just as he, I sensed, stood and stared at the back of my head.

And now you're going to have to REALLY concentrate – because what happened next is so completely ridiculous that everything up until now will seem quite sane and normal.

KATHY says:

That doesn't seem possible.

TOM says:

As I sat at the table I began to wonder if anyone else had ever had a problem like this – if I was the only one who'd ever seen the little bald man. Perhaps he was a common phantom. And as I thought that the doorbell rang. Now you know how I've lived my life these last years; I've cut myself off from everyone, even you, my dear. So as I stood to go to the door, I knew it could only be the paper boy looking for payment: my only human contact in the week. As I

crossed the hall, the thought of newspapers gave me an idea. I had a photograph of the little bald man – who flickered at my shoulder, even as I walked – why not simply place an ad? An ad in the paper! His photograph and "Have you seen this man?" This was the thought in my head as I pulled open the door.

A man I'd never seen stood there. "Hello, saw your ad! I'm the Doctor, I'm here to help."

I stared. He was holding a copy of a newspaper, showing me the very ad I'd just composed in my head. The same photograph I had just selected. The words: "Have you seen this man?" My phone number!

He was looking at me, frowning. "This is your ad, right?"

I believe I gaped at him. "Yes. It's mine, it's definitely mine."

"What's the problem then?"

"I haven't placed it yet!"

"Ah!" He glanced at his watch. "Well if you wouldn't mind placing it a bit sharpish, that'd be good. Otherwise there's gonna be a nasty big time paradox and most of the galaxy's gonna unravel. Again. And I didn't half get in trouble the last time, people get so cross."

He shifted his gaze slightly, looking at a point just over my shoulder. "Right, baldy! Make yourself scarce! And pack your bags, it's moving day!"

There was a scurry of feet behind me and I turned to see a tiny figure darting out of sight into the living room. When I turned again the Doctor had pushed his way into the house and was walking towards the kitchen.

"Tell you what, I'll place the ad. Better not leave it to you, what with the end of the universe and all that gubbins."

He was in the kitchen now. He pulled up a chair, banged his feet on the table. "Right then. You've got questions. Don't blame you, I'd have questions. In fact, I do have questions. For a start, what about this house?"

"What about it?"

"Well it's rubbish, isn't it? Look at it. Filthy, dusty, you've hardly had a visitor here for –" he took a big sniff, "– oh, ten years, I'd say. That about right?"

"Yes," I said, "About ten."

"Why?" It was such a blunt question, I was suddenly at a loss.

"I prefer not to."

"What, one day, about ten years ago, you just decided you wanted to be on your own, all day, every day?"

It seemed ridiculous the way he said it, but I could only answer: "Yes."

"Go out much?"

"As little as I can. I have agoraphobia."

"Fear of open spaces. Okay, wild guess – you suddenly developed a fear of open spaces ten years ago?"

My voice seemed very faint in my own ears. "Yes."

"Don't you see? Doesn't make sense, does it? You're being manipulated. Low-level psychic manipulation. And as a result you've spent ten years alone in a big house with a Floof."

"What," I asked, "is a Floof?"

"It's small, and it's bald, and I'm coming to that. Ten years, barely any human contact, and it's never even struck you as odd."

"My wife," I said, "I speak to my wife every day!"

He looked surprised for a moment. "Your wife. Of course, wedding ring, should've noticed. Okay then, let's meet the wife. Wheel on the missus!"

I took him to this computer.

"You speak to your wife on Instant Messenger?"

"Every day!"

"Well that's a poor excuse for a relationship – and I'm not usually one to talk. Why don't you live together?"

I looked at him. I had no answer.

"You're married," he persisted, "Why don't you live together?"

I just stood there and kept looking at him.

"Well?" he said.

There was a roaring in my ears. I felt as if the whole world around me was shifting into a new shape, and I could see it clearly for the first time in so many years. And I didn't understand anything I saw.

Kathy, why don't we live together?

KATHY says:

I don't know. I can't remember.

TOM says:

We're married. Why do we only talk on the computer?

KATHY says:

I don't know. I can't remember.

TOM says:

We were married, we were happy. Why did we split up??

KATHY says:

I don't know. I can't remember.

TOM says:

Neither can I. Oh, Kathy, neither can I.

The Doctor had his hands on my shoulders, steadying me as my world spun.

"It's the Floof. It can control and limit your thoughts, so long as it stays close."

"What," I begged, "please, for God's sake, tell me, WHAT is a Floof?"

"Odd little creatures," said the Doctor, settling back on to his chair. "No one really knows where they came from, because they're pretty much impossible to study. But where there are humans, or humanoids, there are Floofs. Millions of them, usually. But no one ever knows a thing about them, because there's an ability that evolution can throw up that no one, but no one, can ever learn anything about. The super-evolved ability to hide."

"To hide??"

"A Floof can stand in a bare room full of a hundred people, all looking in every direction, all searching for it – and find the one spot no one's looking at. You can be alone in a room with a Floof, and spinning round and round trying to see it – and the Floof will just spin faster. However fast you turn to look, a Floof has moved away faster. Just a tiny movement in the corner of your eye. People get used to it, think it's normal. They hear a creak, and they say it's the house settling! What's that mean, 'house settling'? No such thing as 'house settling'!

They get a prickling on the back on their necks, they think their hairs are standing on end. What's that about? Hair doesn't stand! It's a Floof breathing right behind you."

"But what do they want, these Floofs?"

"Nothing much. Mischevious more than anything. They'll nick your pens, your socks, move around your car keys – they love all that. You write a phone number on a scrap of paper, they'll whip it away soon as you turn round."

His face turned darker.

"But sometimes… well, sometimes they get a bit possessive. As in your case. Your Floof has cut you off from the rest of the world. It wants you all to itself."

"The rest of the world, except my wife." I corrected him.

He frowned, and looked to the computer.

"You only ever talk on Instant Messenger," he said. "No letters, no phone calls?"

"I never write letters. And I hate the phone."

"Anything else at all? Emails?"

"I don't have an internet connection."

He stared at me. "Say that again."

"I don't have an internet connection, I've never had an internet connection."

He was rising from his chair, his eyes burning at me. "Say it again, and this time listen to what you're saying"!

"I don't have a –"

The words died in my mouth.

Kathy! Kathy, my love! How can I be talking to you on Instant Messenger if I DON'T HAVE AN INTERNET CONNECTION.

KATHY says:

Where am I? Tom, please, tell me now, where am I? I don't seem to be anywhere. I'm just words! How can I just be words?? WHERE AM I?

TOM says:

The Doctor spent the rest of the day looking for you. By the evening he emerged from the cellar looking grim.

KATHY says:

Why would he be looking for me in the cellar? What would I be doing in the cellar?

TOM says:

He found you buried under the wine racks. He said you'd been dead for at least ten years. The Floof killed you. I'm sorry. I'm so, so sorry.

KATHY says:

But I'm not dead. I'm here. How can I be dead if I'm still here??

TOM says:

You're not here. You're not even really Kathy. The Doctor explained it to me, once he'd examined the computer. The Floof knew he could control me only to a limited degree. He might make me forget why we'd parted, but he couldn't remove my desire to talk to you. But they're smart, Floofs. What he did was he created another you. He programmed the computer with everything he knew about you – which was a lot, he was the perfect spy – and created a program to respond exactly the way you would. You're not Kathy. You've never been Kathy. You're a subroutine that THINKS it's Kathy.

KATHY says:

That's not true. I'm me, I'm Kathy, I can feel it!

TOM says:

Okay. Then describe the room you're in.

KATHY says:

The room has three yellow walls and one blue wall. The room is 12 feet by 8 feet. The room has one door. The room has no windows. The room has four lights. The room has seven chairs. The room has two light switches.

TOM says:

You see? Exactly what you said before. The real Kathy never saw the room the computer sits in now, it was a cupboard back then. So with nothing else to go on, you're pulling information about the room from somewhere else on the computer. That's why it's just a list of facts. That's all the computer knows, so it's all you know.

KATHY says:

I'm me. I know I'm me. If I wasn't me, why would you even bother talk to me?

TOM says:

Let me finish my story.

KATHY says:

Why bother finishing it? You don't even think I'm real! You think I'm a computer!

TOM says:

Just let me finish the story.

KATHY says:

If you must.

TOM says:

Once the Doctor had found your body, he changed. Before he had seemed so light, so jolly. Now he was thunder. And he spoke like thunder too.

"Floof!" he roared. "Floof, come here and stand in my sight!!"

Nothing stirred in the house.

"Listen to me, Floof! You can hide from him, but nothing can hide from me. Listen to my voice! I'm angry now. But, oh, I can get angrier. So come here and STAND IN MY SIGHT!"

And suddenly he was there, like he just folded himself out of a corner. The Floof, in full view. The tiny bald man who had killed my love.

The Doctor looked down at him. "Here's the thing. Here's the deal. You took a life. So I'm taking yours."

The Floof said nothing for a moment. Then, softly: "We are very difficult to kill."

"Didn't say I'd kill you, I said I'd take your life. And your life –" and he turned and pointed at me "– is him."

The Floof looked at me; lost, alarmed, I could almost have felt sorry for him. "You can't. No, please. He's mine."

"Not any more," said the Doctor, "He's leaving. In my TARDIS, where you can't follow. And you can do what you like. You can mope around this house and pine for a hundred years, for all I care. Suits me, every town needs a haunted house. And I can't see anyone else moving into this dump. You'll be alone, that's your punishment. But you listen to me. I'll be watching. I'm always watching. And if you harm another living soul, I'll be back."

He glanced at me. "Right. Let's go. Don't pack, I'll lend you a toothbrush."

He was already halfway to the door.

"I can't," I said.

He turned. He had a face made for surprise.

I looked at the computer. "I can't leave Kathy."

He stared and stared. The Floof looked at me in hope and wonder.

"That's not Kathy!" He seemed close to exploding. "I explained! That's a computer program that THINKS it's Kathy."

"For the last ten years, that program has been my wife. I will not leave it here alone."

"Well, we'll switch off the computer!"

"We will not switch off the computer!"

"Fine, we'll leave it running!"

"She'll be alone!"

"She's not a she, she's a subroutine!"

"That's no subroutine, that's my wife!"

He stared at me for a long, wondering moment. And then he gave the biggest sigh ever. "Humans!" he said. "Honestly, you humans. I should just have got a pet."

KATHY says:

Oh, my love. You stayed. You did, you stayed! You stayed for me!

TOM says:

No, of course not, my love. The Doctor was right and he convinced me in the end. I couldn't stay, not just for a computer program. I would've stayed for the real Kathy. But, my love, you're not the real Kathy.

KATHY says:

If I'm not the real Kathy, why are you here, why are you talking to me?

TOM says:

Oh, haven't you guessed? This is what the Doctor did for you. For me, for both of us.

KATHY says:

What are you talking about? My question stands. If I'm not the real Kathy, why are you still here?

TOM says:

Because I'm not the real Tom.

KATHY says:

I don't understand. You're scaring me again. Who are you then?

TOM says:

Ask me where I am.

KATHY says:

Where are you?

TOM says:

The room has three yellow walls and one blue wall. The room is 12 feet by 8 feet. The room has one door. The room has no windows. The room has four lights The room has seven chairs. The room has two light switches.

THE END